TRAP BOY

A NOVEL BY
BARBIE SCOTT

This Novel is dedicated to:
Vanessa Vasquez & Skylar White

Prologe *(Pedro)*

"Nooo Mijo"

"BJ!" Pedro shouted in hopes that the one year child could be found within the Atlantic Ocean. He swam to the bottom of the ocean several times in hope that he would find the young boys body soon or that it would come afloat. He looked around in a panic when a sudden movement just a couple of feet away caught his eye. "Finally" he thought, Pedro swam as quickly as he could. His heart felt a pang of relief as he grabbed BJ who appeared to be unconscious, and swam to the surface to pull him from under the water. He observed him closely for any injuries and only noticed a slightly deep gash above his right eye. He tried his hardest to stay afloat as he began to give BJ CPR. "Come on Papi, no se puede morir Mijo." Pedro said pumping BJ's chest. He was in such a frantic, but because of his past life as a hit man, he was taught to never panic. Once the young boy began to choke, he said a silent prayer, thanking God. He quickly put him back into the water to keep the young child warm, but making sure to hold him closely. Looking out into the ocean, Pedro was devastated. The many bodies that floated at least a hundred yards away from him belonged to his dear friends. What crushed his soul was seeing Ms. Lopez with half her face blown off and bleeding profoundly from where he didn't know. Cash was dead, Esco was dead, their entire crew was now dead and even, Rosa, the love of Pedro's life; DEAD!

Prior to the explosion, Pedro held BJ in is his arms as he enjoyed the wedding of Cash Lopez and Nino Carter, that was being held on the Yacht. "Candy" BJ fussed looking over at the candy table Cash had sat up at the end of the Yacht. As soon as the explosion transpired, the impact knocked Pedro and BJ in the ocean causing them to quickly sink. BJ was thrown from Pedro's arms but Pedro knew he wasn't far.

Knowing that Ms. Lopez was now dead, pained him like the day his wife and child were killed. Years ago Pedro was a paid hitman who worked for some top Cartels. He made plenty money doing the job but no money in the world could replace the amount of pain he felt over losing his wife and son. Right after the devastating news, he went to work for Ms. Lopez who ran a multi million dollar drug empire, as her private hitman. Pedro and Ms. Lopez had been friends for years so she welcomed him with open arms. She had a small four bedroom home built near her swimming pool of her Mansion for Pedro and treated him like family. Cash was a very young girl when Pedro came to work for Ms. Lopez, but he knew from the first time he'd met her, she would be nothing to toy with. He had helped her clean up the mess of her first body. Cash was only eleven or twelve as he recalled, when the young girl murdered one of Ms. Lopez's workers. Pedro was the one who was there to comfort her and also take the wrap. Many years later Cash had grown into a beautiful young lady, who did great in school and had career goals, until, Ms. Lopez was knocked by the Federal Police and was taken into custody. Cash stepped up to the plate and began to run the drug empire, up until the day Ms. Lopez was reunited with the streets. Just in the short years of Ms. Lopez being home, so much had happened within the empire. There were, snakes, snitches and deceivers amongst their circle that was quickly put to ease. Ms. Lopez had began to run her empire once again, and Cash had fell in love with one of Miami's top Kingpins, whom she birth BJ with. Today was the day of Cash's wedding and things were going pretty good up into this point. The first wedding Cash and Nino had, ended in a deadly blood bath, due to the Cartels retaliation. So today Cash decided to do something a little more exclusive. A private destination wedding in the bahamas. There she hoped they couldn't be touched. Pedro knew that The Cartel was capable of anything but he pushed the thoughts away with keeping faith.

Now he was left alone once again and he knew this day would forever haunt him. He looked at BJ who was shivering in his arms and kissed the top of his head. He was thankful that he saved one memory from his life. He would take BJ in as his own and show him the two tools in life; To get money and handle the respect that will be bestowed upon him being the grandson of Ms. Lopez, and the son of Cash and Nino. He knew with the right guidance, the power BJ already held would keep the legacy of the Lopez/Carter empire ALIVE.

CHAPTER 1 *(16 years later) Brooklyn Jr.*

"Make every blow count"

"Whap!" Pedro's punch connected with BJ's jaw line. BJ quickly shook it off, and focused on his prey. With ease, he studied Pedro long and hard then went in for the two punch combination to the ribs. Landing each punch he grinned at his accomplishment.

"Come on old man, you ain't losing your touch are you?" BJ taunted with Pedro as he circled around him. His legs were placed firmly to the black mat and he kept his guards up fiercely. With a quick kick to the leg, BJ instantly fell. He quickly jumped back to his feet and began circling Pedro again. The knock down had BJ's blood boiling so his mind only instructed him to fire back.

Make every blow count and you could walk away; otherwise you may be carried away. The only rule in fighting is to live Papi. Pedro's words played over and over in his mind. Jab, Jab, Hook, BJ quickly put Pedro on his back. The sound of Pedro's coughs alarmed BJ and caused him to quickly run over. He kneeled down besides Pedro in fear that he had hurt the old man. With a quick head lock, Pedro quickly flipped BJ over and now had him on his back. He looked BJ in the eyes,

"Never take your eyes off the prize Mijo." Pedro said in his strong accent. BJ simply nodded in agreement. "Don't be afraid to hit first, and when you do, hit hard. Remember, you are fighting because this is the best and only option. You don't know the other person's intentions fully, and you never can. What you can do is survive -- it is your right to not be killed or harmed by another person. The spinal cord, the windpipe and the two carotid arteries Papi, your attacker may be three times your size, but if you take away even one of these functions, the fight is over." BJ payed close attention and made sure to make a mental note to everything Pedro had said. Even though BJ had heard everything he said a million and one times, he was a smart wise boy so he knew to take heed to every single word.

Since BJ was four years old, Pedro had been training him to survive. Pedro was all BJ had and that wouldn't be for long. Pedro was a very old man, but because he continued to work out, he didn't look his age one bit. Lately Pedro had been getting sick, but he always brushed it off as to just old age. He knew his time was coming but he made sure that BJ would be able to survive on his on. Pedro never showed BJ the ropes to the drug game, however he taught the young boy how to fight and shoot a gun if need be. BJ was actually a pretty good kid, but he did contain lots of his parents ways. He had a attitude like his father with a very cocky demeanor like his mother. The long locks that hung from his head only added to him looking like a spit image of Brooklyn Nino Carter Sr. His big round eyes, is what reminded Pedro of Cash and his smooth caramel skin tone is what he had inherited because of Ms. Lopez's Puerto Rican descent.

Watching BJ with his shirt off he couldn't help but laugh. BJ held a very thuggish demeanor exactly like his father with a swag that would soon drive the young girls wild. He had snuck off and got a few tattoos. He had a collage of angel wings on his back along with his mother and fathers portraits. On his neck read RIP Beloved

Abuelita and Ms. Lopez's name. On his chest he had Pedro's named engraved. He had gotten the tattoo because he always said that Pedro would forever be in his heart. BJ loved Pedro with every ounce of him. He was very grateful for Pedro saving his life and taking him in as his own child.

"Come on BJ let's go eat and get you ready for school." Pedro said walking into the house. BJ followed closely behind because he had worked up a serious appetite. Tomorrow was BJ's first day of his senior year and BJ was slightly excited. He was also nervous because he wasnt very social.

The deed to Ms. Lopez's mansion was in Pedro's name making him now the owner. In fear that the Cartel would find out him and BJ were alive, he simply moved them to a beach house in a secluded area. The beach house was segregated from the rest of the beach with a huge gate closing it into its own private spacing. Once BJ turned eighteen, it was up to him to chose to occupy the mansion, but the beach house would always be his private escape. Pedro knew that many years had passed so no one would probably recognize BJ but just to be on the safe side, he had trained him to protect himself. Since a kid, Pedro had gotten BJ home schooled. Because he didn't want to deprive the boy of having a normal teenage life; He now chose to let him finish off his schooling on a public campus.

***

Walking into his High School, BJ was a bit nervous but held his head up. He wasn't scared, however, he hadn't been around this many kids his age ever in his life. BJ didn't really plan on making any friends but the idea of feeling free made him feel as if he had missed out on a lot. Walking through the hallway, it was like all eyes were rested on the new kid. The guys watched him in awe and the girls were admiring his every move. From his shoes to the cuban link chain on his neck, the kids assumed that his parents were rolling in dough. Little did they know the young man had his own money and plenty of it. He had a Audi A8 parked right outside of the campus, that everyone probably thought belonged to a teacher. Pedro had taught BJ how to drive when he was thirteen so he was now well experienced. Taking BJ to a car lot, he expected him to get something suitable for a young man, but when his eyes landed on the Audi, Pedro couldn't do anything but laugh.

Upon walking to class, BJ noticed a young boy who was draped in jewelry but what caught his eye was the Paul Newman Rolex watch he wore. BJ knew that watch costed an obscene amount of money because he had one exactly like it. He also payed attention to how the women flocked on the guy but with his smooth and laid back demeanor he simply smiled and ignored the women. “Excuse me, are you Brooklyn Carter?” the teacher asked BJ and pulled him into the classroom. All eyes were on him as he nodded his head. “It’s so nice to meet you I'm Mrs. Elaine Pendergrass. And I'm your new teacher.” she extended her hand. “Nice to meet you.” BJ smiled and went to take a seat. With the manors that BJ had, he could win the heart of any girl, woman or child. That trait he had gotten from Cash. She was well mannered and very polite even through the eyes of a killer. For a woman, Cash was a straight beast. She would wine and dine you and in less than a half of second, you'd be laying in your own blood.

The morning came and went pretty quickly. It was now lunch and BJ really didn't know what to do with himself. He wanted to leave campus but didn't really know where to go. He knew where the mall was located but he figured he wouldn't make it back in time.

"BJ Carter." his name was announced over the intercom. Puzzled, he scrunched his face as to why was he being called into the office. Turning around he bumped into a chick knocking her books to the ground.

"My bad ma." He spoke and the beauty before him only smiled. She bent down to pick up her belongings with not much care that she had been nearly knocked down.

"Can you show me where the office at?" He asked not knowing which way to go.

"Its down the hall and out that door." She pointed.

"Once you go out that door, it's on the right." She smiled.

"Thanks." He walked off without another word. *She pretty as a muthafucka.* He thought as he walked down the hall. On his short walk he couldn't help but think of how pretty she was. Her hair was long and bone straight with a middle part. He could tell it was her natural hair. She was a tad bit light skin but not to light past his likings. She had a nice little frame and her smile was enough to brighten anybody's day. What really drew him in was the girl's innocence. She had a shy like attitude and that made him want her little ass. However, he would fall back for now.

BJ wasn't into wife-ing girls, but he was very much experienced. He had met a few girls on the beach and with all the privacy Pedro allowed him, he would take them up to his room and fuck them until he left them limp. BJ's life didn't revolve around women. He would simply sex them then push them to the side. However, there was one girl that just wouldn't leave him alone; Kamela. She was a real bugaboo and that shit annoyed BJ's soul. She was a really pretty girl but with the experience she possessed at such a young age let him know she had been fucked plenty of times and that made him not want any parts of her.

When he walked into the office, Manuel, one of Pedro's friends held a bag in his hand. He smiled when he saw BJ and handed him the bag. "Good looking Manuel." BJ retrieved the bag. He quickly left and headed back out the door to find a spot to sit and eat. Finding a cool little shade tree with a table, he sat down and began to tear open the bag. Pedro had sent him some Lobster Pasta, grilled Tilapia and garlic bread. He opened the little container and he smiled widely looking over the salad. It had cucumbers, eggs, cheese and tomatoes just how he liked it. There was a separate container that he opened curiously, because he had everything he need already. It was a Rock lobster with melted garlic butter. BJ rubbed his hands together and he was now in food heaven. Biting into his lobster, he heard a voice from behind him. He turned around and it was the guy from his first period class.

"Damn my nigga slow down." The guy said making BJ laugh.

"My bad, a nigga hungry." BJ said picking up his napkin to wipe his hands.

"Im Calvin but everyone call me Cali."

"I'm Brooklyn but everyone calls me BJ"

"Man you rich or something?" Cali said eyeing BJ's meal.

“Nah, not at all.” BJ kept it simple. And besides his lifestyle wasn’t anybody's business.

“Shit I can't tell, nigga you got Lobster at school.” Again the fellas laughed.

“Its yo first day huh?” Cali asked and BJ nodded. Normally Cali wouldn't talk to other guys because most of the niggas at school hated on him. They hated everything about him from the way he dressed to his cockiness. What they hated most, was how all the women wanted him. Looking over BJ's whole attire he could tell BJ had his own everything so a hater is what he wasn't.

The guys made small talk until the bell rang. BJ had to admit Cali seemed really cool so they exchanged instagrams so they could stay up with each other out of school. BJ had told Cali that he didn't party, so Cali made it his business to enlighten BJ on a few clubs that they could hit up without any ID. They made plans to function together sooner rather than later.

CHAPTER 2 *(Brooklyn Jr.)*

"Wake up every morning feeling blessed up..."

"How was school my boy?" Pedro asked the moment BJ was in the door.

"It was real cool Papa." Bj said calling Pedro by the name he had been calling him since a baby.

"How many girls you get?" Pedro laughed knowing BJ was such a ladies man.

"Hahaha. I ain't got none. But man its this one chick, she bad as fuck..I mean hell." BJ said correcting himself. No Matter how cool Pedro was, he would respect him.

"So what happen?"

"Nothing she just showed me to the office. I didn't even get her name."

"Well you'll see her tomorrow."

"I can't wait too. I met a cool dude though. His name Cali. He pretty much showed me around the school. Nigga was fly like me too" BJ boasted and they both laughed.

"That's good Papi you can't be a loner all your life. You're smart enough to not be a follower so get you some friends man."

"I know. We got each other instagrams."

"Okay thats cool. I'm going to go laydown. My back been hurting me lately and the pinche medicine not working."

"Okay. I'll be in my room. I'm about to knock this homework out then shower and shit." Pedro couldn't help but laugh as he walked into his room. BJ was growing into a man and soon would be eighteen.

After BJ had taken his shower and knocked out his homework, he hopped on instagram. He went to Cali's page in hopes he would find the beauty from school. Cali was very popular on campus so he figured he would have every girl in school on his account. Searching through Cali's many friends, he stared closely at each picture. Halfway through the friends list, he landed right on the girl's profile pic. He clicked onto the girls page and "*damn*" he cursed himself because her page was private. He went back to Cali's page and showed him some love by liking a few pics. Soon after he had a dm. When he opened it, it was Cali, telling him to call with his number attached. BJ quickly dialed the number and waited for Cali to answer.

"Sup BJ?"

"Whats da deal man?"

"Shit just got to the crib. You in for the night?"

"Hell yeah. I just finished this work from Mrs. Pendergrass now I'm bout to play Madden."

"Damn nigga you balling and smart." Cali said and they both laughed.

"You a fool my nigga. Aye what's up with ol girl from the school? I don't know her name but her insta is Aaliyah with three H's."

"That's Aaliyah bad ass. Good luck with that one. I fucked almost every girl in school except her. I think her little stuck up ass a virgin."

"Is that right?" BJ smiled. Just the thought of her being a virgin made him want her more than before.

"Aaliyah aint fucking with yo black ass." Cali laughed.

"Watch me work nigga. Give me less than a week I bet you I'll have that ass."

"We gone see." They both laughed.

After talking with Cali for nearly two hours BJ had disconnected the call and began to play his game. The entire game he was getting his ass whooped because his mind was elsewhere. He wondered what was up with Aaliyah and if she had a boyfriend. Just because she was a virgin didn't mean she didn't have a nigga. He just prayed that who ever he was, he wouldn't be getting the goods.

The next morning BJ woke up with more to look forward too. His iffy feelings about going to public school had changed thanks to his new homie; he had made shit a breeze for him. He headed into the shower and began his daily routine. Once he was done and completely dressed, he headed towards his room. Walking past Pedro's room he heard him coughing and it sounded bad. BJ quickly ran to the kitchen and grabbed a bottled water. He went back into the room and handed Pedro the bottled water.

"You good Papa?"

"Thanks Mijo. Yeah I'm fine, you head to school before you're late."

"Okay. If you need something call me."

"Okay thanks."

The sound of Pedro's cough made BJ want to stay home and monitor him. He hated to leave his Papa in such condition but he knew Pedro wouldn't take him missing school lighly. He hoped in his ride and turned on his "Dream Chaser 4" CD then slowly backed out his garage. BJ loved Meek Mill's music, listening to the lyrics to "Blessed Up" he bopped his head as he made his way towards campus.

I got God watching over me from court side,
ballin like I'm Jordan because I'm blessed up.
And niggas want me gone but I'm still alive,
wake up every morning feeling blessed up.

With all the stories he had heard from Pedro, he wished he could have met his parents. Listening to the song, BJ, felt as blessed to be here but he longed to be in his mother's arms. Putting the pedal to the metal, he tried blocking the thoughts of his parents out of his mind. He switched the song and pulled out his phone to call Cali. Right then he spotted Cali hopping out of a brand new Challenger. BJ exited his car, hit his alarm, then made his way over to Cali who was already indulging in a conversation with two chicks. BJ couldn't help but laugh because they weren't even on campus five minutes and Cali was already being sweated by some dark skin chick with a long weave. The other chick mugged BJ the moment he walked up.

"Top of the am my nigga." Cali gave BJ a pound.

"Damn Cali who's this?" the dark skin girl asked.

"Why?" BJ replied not amused by the women.

"Why? Wow that's rude." she said mugging him. He ignored her and walked off but telling Cali he'd catch up with him, leaving the girls angry. A smirk crept upon his face as he walked off not giving two fucks at how the women felt. BJ wasn't the typical nice boy. Don't let his laid back and well mannered demeanor confuse you. He hated thot bitches and he had a slick ass mouth. Out of all the women he'd seen on campus, only one caught his eye and he wasn't about to chase her either.

***

When the bell finally rung, BJ rushed out of his class room. As much as he would have loved to stay behind, he wanted to get home to check on Pedro. He walked out of the school in a hurried pace but stopping in his tracks at what he saw before him. Aaliyah was standing by the gym hugged up with a guy. BJ hadn't seen the guy on campus so he assumed the guy didn't attend their school. He also appeared to be a little older than BJ so he was sure the guy didn't attend. Walking past Aaliyah and the guy, BJ nodded his head back to Aaliyah who had waved.

"Fuck you nodding at?" The guy said before BJ was out of ears reach. BJ turned around to make sure he was talking to him. When he seen that the guy was staring him square dead in the eyes, his blood began to boil. BJ had a really short fuse and didn't take shit from no one. "Fuck you mean who I'm nodding at." BJ shot forcefully. Aaliyah grabbed the guy's arm but he snatched it away. He walked into BJ's space but not close enough to get caught with a sucker punch. *Even a 250-pound man made of solid muscle will stop fighting if he can't breathe, which is why you must concentrate the full force of your attack on the face and neck area.* Pedro's words played in BJ's head. The guy was indeed much bigger than him but to BJ that didn't mean shit. As bad as he wanted to just walk away, he knew the guy was only showing out in front of his chick. Little did the nigga know, BJ was one not to be reckoned with.

BJ knew what he was capable of, and this was the reason he didn't indulge in friends. His mindset was much different from your typical seventeen year old and his hands were very much skilled. It was like a instant reaction when the guy stepped a foot closer. Two quick Jabs and a hook to the windpipe caused the guy to fold instantly. Before he knew it, he was snatched back and Cali's foot was landing on top of the guys head. Aaliyah stood off to the side, and the sound of her cries were the only thing that broke BJ from his trance.

"Ms. Green coming!" a student yelled referring to the principle. BJ and Cali quickly walked away and leaving the guy nearly unconcious. Before walking off, he had shot Aaliyah one last look. He hated to see her cry, but he also hated to be talked to as if he was some sort of bitch.

Walking into the lot with Cali in tow, they both stood by BJ's Audi and began to make small talk. BJ had so many questions but he didn't want to seem thirsty. After what he had seen today, all thoughts of Aaliyah were now pushed out of his mind. *Bitch aint no virgin.* He thought to himself and was now cool on her.

"Yo my nigga what the fuck you was in the army or something?" Cali laughed with a dead serious tone. The move he had seen BJ put on the guy was something that had come from some sort of combat. Little did Cali know, he had in deed been trained and by one of the best hitmen in town.

"Nah. a nigga just know how to fight." BJ kept it simple. Though he liked Cali, he would always keep up the brick wall he had formed around himself. BJ's motto was *Trust No One* and he would live by it. He had heard a lot about his parents from his Papa, so he knew that he had to move cautiously.

"So whats up wanna roll to my crib?" Cali said bringing him from his daze.

"I gotta roll to the house and check on my pops."

"Oh okay. Well hit me when you get online so I could whoop yo ass in Madden."

"You mean so I could whoop yo ass nigga." They both laughed. The sound of yelling got the guys attention. They turned to where the noise was coming from and noticed it was a older man screaming down Aaliyah's throat. The older man was yelling to the top of his lungs as he escorted her into a limousine.

"Damn who's that?" BJ looked at Cali.

"That's her grandpa. Nigga mean as shit. They don't let her do shit. She can't even stay after school." Cali shook his head.

"Damn thats crazy. Aight though I'm bout to take my ass home." BJ dapped Cali and hopped in his ride. Pulling out the lot, he gave Aaliyah one last look as he drove past the limo. She looked so sad and right then he could tell that she wasn't happy with her living situation.

CHAPTER 3 *(Aaliyah)*

"The NewGuy"

In the backseat of the limousine, Aaliyah rode in complete silence. Her grandfather was giving her the third degree about being in the face of some thug. As bad as she wanted to protest his actions she chose to remain silent. She hated how he treated her but wouldn't dare question his authority. She told herself time and time, that once she finished school she would leave his home and never come back. Her grandfather was too strict for her likings. She had one friend that he had finally accepted after two years and he would die before he let her date. She felt as if she was being held as a prisoner not being able to do the things most girls her age did.

Aaliyahs mother had died when she was just a baby so she was stuck being raised by her grandfather who was the head of a Cartel. Everytime she would ask about her father, her grandfather would simply say he was dead. For some reason, she figured it was more to the story. At just the mention of Aaliyahs dad, her grandfather's blood boiled, so after years of asking, she had finally left the subject alone. She didn't have a name nor a face, however, she wished that one day she would be rescued by him. Aaliyah knew that her grandfather wanted what was best for her, but sometimes he was a bit to overprotective. Like now.

She couldn't have a car like most teenagers. He would send someone to pick her up from school. She couldn't even leave the house without guards and male friends were not tolerated. She was actually shocked when he had finally agreed to let her go to a public school. For many years she had been in an all girls school that only consisted of ten students.

Aaliyah's family was pretty wealthy. She had everything a child would ever want but freedom. She lived in a mansion the size of a castle and her bedroom alone was the size of a typical two bedroom apartment. Her grandfather had made sure to provide her with anything she desired and more, but to Aaliyah she just wanted to be free.

Pulling up to her mansion, she sighed silently because she was bored with her lifestyle. *What good was having money if you couldn't have fun*. She spent most of her days talking to the family's maid and entertaining herself in her home. Growing up with the maid, Blanca, Aaliyah felt the comfort from the older woman. She often told Aaliyah that she understood how she felt, but she also helped her understand as to why the family was so over protective. Aaliyah's grandpa Mario was a known drug dealer who had made enemies with some powerful people. Over the years, he'd practically murdered all his alias, however he still made sure his grandchild was protected.

Aaliyah exited the car and made her way into her bedroom still feeling embarrassed. She had noticed BJ and Cali near their vehicles when her grandfather decided to make a mockery out of her. She had already felt the embarrassment from the beat down that BJ had giving to her ex and then her grandpa only made matters worse.

Aaliyah and Timothy had been secretly dating for some time. They had broken up because of course she wasn't giving up the goods. She had been hearing from her best friend that he was fooling around but until she had seen it for herself she wouldn't trip. The chick Timothy started getting serious with, had sent Aaliyah a few videos of them making out. The video of the chick sucking his dick is what blew her back the most. Like all men, he tried to deny the allegations but the proof was in the videos. Aaliyah had left him alone but he wouldn't let up that easy, like today. Timothy had popped up to the school trying to plead his case but Aaliyah was unfazed by his presence. BJ so happened to walk by the two as they were indulging in a friendly hug. She hated that BJ had to see that because in all honesty she was crushing on him something serious. Timothys reaction to BJ acknowledging her, escalated into something that didn't even have to happen. She had been warning Tim about his slick mouth but he never would listen. Seeing BJ, beat the shit out of Tim, only made her like him more. The fire in his eyes and the danger he posed, made her crave the young thug. Now she prayed BJ wouldn't be upset with her. *Sigh.*

Laying on her bed, she pulled out her iphone 7. She went to her instagram and went straight to Cali's page. She wasn't sure if BJ was into social media but she would soon find out. As soon as the page loaded, there was a pic of BJ and Cali standing by the lunch tables at school. She smiled at how they were posing and also happy that his name was tagged in the post. BJ was the new guy around and she was crushing extremely hard. Besides the name brand clothing he wore and his sexy demeanor, she could tell he was a genuine guy. It was something about BJ that drew her in, however, she knew he was out of her league. If he didn't have a girlfriend, she was sure he had plenty women flocking to him left and right. He seemed very mature for his age and with the dreads that hung past his shoulders, he looked older than what he was.

Aaliyah clicked on BJ's instagram and his page was private. She was nervous to send him a request so she dm's him instead.

DM: Hey BJ I really apologize about today.

Was all she said. She waited for a few moments and he had finally responded.

DM: You good.

Was all he replied and she was quickly saddened. She went back to her own page and began browsing through her newsfeed. Her heart lit up, on the screen letting her know she had a notification. When she clicked on the heart, a friend request awaited her from BJ. She smiled to herself and quickly accepted but making sure to follow him back. Soon after, her notifications blew up because BJ had liked a ton of her pictures. She went to his page and showed the same love. He had some really great pics of him on the beach and walking through the mall. The picture that drew her in, was the one of him in a pair of boxing gloves while looking coldly into the camera. He had a scar above his right eye that gave him a sexy demeanor. Rubbing her hand across the screen she couldn't help but blush because he was indeed a sight to see. She wanted to comment on the pic but thought against it. Aaliyah was far from thirsty so she didn't want to appear as some hoe like all the other girls.

“Aaliyah.” her door opened and she quickly dropped her phone. When she saw that it was Blanca, she sighed in relief.

“Hey Blanca.”

“Hey Mija. you hungry?”

“No I'm fine thank you.”

“Ok call me if you want comida.”

“Okay.” Aaliyah smiled. She was so grateful for Ms. Blanca because she held every secret. Mario was so strict, Aaliyah wasn't able to even have a cellular phone. Blanca was the one who had got it for her and made her promise to withhold the secret. Laying back on her bed, Aaliyah went through every last picture BJ had on his page. She knew she had to go shower for the next day but she was so caught up on the new kid, she told herself everything else could wait.

***

After Aaliyah's shower, she hopped on the phone and dialed her best and only friend Venicia. She was ready for a little gossip about the guys at school. They often got a kick out of how in love Venicia was with Cali. She had been crushing on him since she gave him the goods but he was such a ladies man, he wouldn't make her his main chick. Venicia had missed the first two days of school so Aaliyah wanted to fill her in on the new guy. On the fourth ring her voice blared cheerfully through the phone.

“Bestfrienddd”

“Heyyy Best Friend”

“I hope your coming to school tomorrow.”

"Hell yeah I'm coming and what's been going on because you sound awfully cheerful?" Venicia asked hearing the enthusiasm in her friend's voice.

"So there's this new guy" Aaliyah smirked as if Venicia could see her through the phone.

"Awe shit, he must be a sight for sore eyes if your miss goody too shoes ass is crushing." the girls both laughed.

"He's cute or whatever."

"Ohhh you like him. I could hear it all in your voice Liyah." Again they both laughed.

For the next few hours the girls gossiped on the phone. Venicia began to pry with her million questions about Cali and of course Aaliyah had an ear full for her including the incident with Timothy. For most of the conversation, Aaliyah found herself drifting off with sweet thoughts about the new guy. Tonight she would sleep great and she looked forward to school the next day. *Sweet dreams.*

CHAPTER 4 *(Brooklyn Jr.)*

"Good because you ain't my bitch"

A few days had went by and it was pretty much the same thing. BJ had been going to school and enjoying the time with his new found friend. Cali had come over a couple times, so the guys stayed intertwined into a few games of Madden. Aaliyah reigned heavy on BJ's mind constantly. On campus Aaliyah tried her hardest to make her presence known, but because BJ was still salty about the incident with Timothy, he pretty much gave her the cold shoulder. As much as he would love to get to know her, he had to stand his ground. The innocent girl that he assumed she was, was pretty much out the window which caused him to lose interest. *Just because Cali didn't hit don't mean she ain't fucking.* Were BJ's thoughts whenever he laid eyes on the girl. Watching her as she sat on lunch tables, she looked beautiful to BJ in her baby pink flowy dress. Her hair was bone straight and she would constantly push it out of her face. The slight breeze caused her hair to blow, and her eyes held much innocence. As bad as BJ tried to play it cool, his heart cried out for her touch. He kept stealing glances at her as Cali talked shit about her friend Venicia. Everything Cali said went through one ear and out the other because BJ was lost in outer space.

BJ quickly turned his head when Venicia tapped Aaliyah's shoulder to get up from their table. They walked over to where BJ and Cali sat. Venicia immediately got into Cali's face so Aaliyah took a seat on the other side to give the two some privacy. There was an awkward silence between BJ and Aaliyah so BJ tried to play it cool and make small talk.

"Why you sit yo ass all the way over there?" BJ asked cockily.

"I don't know. Why would you like for me to come over there?" Aaliyah asked flirtatiously.

"Nah you could stay yo ass right there." BJ said and pulled out his cell. Aaliyah watched as he dialed a number then turned his back to talk on the phone.

"Speak to Kamela?" BJ asked into the phone. Aaliyah sat on the side pretending she wasn't jealous but in fact her blood was boiling. *This nigga rude.* She thought to herself then focused her attention on something that didn't hold her interest.

"What time you gone be back. Ima slide through later." BJ smiled holding his phone nestled to his ear. Aaliyah couldn't hear what the caller was saying but the thought of him with another chick hurt her to the core. She stood up from the bench and shot BJ a nasty look then walked off towards her class. When BJ saw her storm off he smirked because he knew his plan had worked. He hated he had to hurt Aaliyah but he wanted her to feel the same feelings he felt when he saw her hugged up days prior.

"What the fuck you do to my friend BJ!" Venicia snapped looking over at BJ.

"Fuck you asking me for? Nobody did shit to that girl" He snapped back and Cali chuckled to himself. Venicia turned around and shot him a meaningful look then snatched her bag off the table.

"Asshole." she stormed by. BJ stuck his tongue out to taunt her, while Cali laughed out making her even angrier.

When the bell rung, the guys made their way to their classes. BJ went to his fifth period gym class while Cali headed in the other direction. Walking through the halls, BJ decided to take the shortcut which was passing by Aaliyah's class. When he made it by the class room, Aaliyah was seated in the back row. He stuck his head in the door an his eyes fell onto Aaliyah who appeared to be focused on the book in front of her. “May I help you?” The teacher asked causing Aaliyha to look up. When they locked eyes, he used his finger to motion for her to come to him. She tilted her head in annoyance because here he was demanding she come to him as if he didn't just disrespect her. “Man bring yo ass here.” BJ mumbled and Aaliyah read his lips. She sighed heavily before getting up from her seat. As bad as she wanted to protest, she didn't want BJ to cause a scene.

Aaliyah walked out of the classroom making sure to close the door behind her. She looked at BJ as if he had lost his mind and the look he gave her was as if he didn't care one bit. Deep down in side Aaliyah was happy he had come to rescue her from the horrible pain she was feeling. After the stunt he had pulled, she was sure to not say anything to him for the rest of their senior year.

“What BJ?”

“Girl don't what me. Stop pouting that shit ain't cute.” He gave her his sexy smirk. Smacking her lips Aaliyah looked at him again annoyed.

“You're really an asshole BJ.”

"Man what you tripping for? Why the fuck you walk away from the table with yo little stank ass attitude huh?" BJ asked stepping into her personal space.

"I'm not tripping off you and yo bitches boy." Aaliyah said trying to sound hip. She was far from the street chick that she was trying to portray. Infact Aaliyah was a straight A student, she did not involve herself in activities that normal kids had indulged in. She had never been to a club nor did she have an idea where to find "the hood" if she tried.

"What you jealous ma? You want daddy? He spoke in a tone that sent shivers down her spine. The cool mint from his breath caused goosebumps down her arms.

"Ain't nobody jealous." She began to bite her bottom lip as she dropped her head in embarrassment. He used his hand to lift her chin and looked her in the eyes without blinking once. He searched her eyes for some sort of desire and it was as if he had gotten lost within them. Quickly shaking the feeling away, BJ stepped back and smirked. "Good because you ain't my bitch." He said and began to walk off. Once again BJ had left Aaliyah hurt and it seemed as if he was getting a kick out of it.

***

After school BJ had went straight home to check on his Papa and do his work. It was friday night and he was ready to get into the swing of things. He had called Cali and just as he figured he was going to a club with his older brother. Bored with his night, BJ pulled out his phone to send Aaliyah a DM. He was getting a kick out of toying with her feelings but tonight he would see how far things would go. He loved the way her body surrendered to him and especially when she pouted like a seven year old.

DM: whats yo number ol big head girl.
DM: (305) 616-6950

BJ wasted no time calling. She quickly answered on the second ring.

"Hello." Aaliyah spoke into the phone in a whisper.

"So whats up? You gone let daddy come thru or what?"

"What do you mean Brooklyn?" She said calling him by his government name. No one had ever called him that, not even his teachers but it was something about the way she said it that melted his heart.

"Exactly what I said. Yes or no? I'm not bout to play games with you ma."

"So what, I say no then you call Kamela?"

"Well yeah." BJ said honestly.

"Well I'm busy anyway so I guess you're gonna have to go fuck that bitch." Aaliyah shot angry. She had had about enough with BJ and after tonight she was done trying. Here it was, one week prior to them meeting and he already had her worked up.

"What you busy with that nigga huh?" BJ shot unable to hide his jealousy.

"Is that what this is about? You know you shouldn't assume things. But anyway, bye BJ go be with your little bitch." Aaliyah disconnected the call. It was something about the way she spoke that changed BJ's whole frame of mind. As horny as he was, he decided to just go lay down. Aaliyah had put something heavy on his mind, and now he regretted even calling.

Laying back on his bed, BJ looked at the portrait of his mother and father that hung on his bedroom wall. The portrait had been delivered to Ms. Lopez's home as a gift from Cash's friend Tiny. It was a wedding gift that Cash never gotten a chance to receive. Tiny was shot and killed right before the wedding by the police along with her soon to be child's father whom was Cash's left hand man Blaze. The feds were coming to indict Blaze on drug trafficking and many more charges that were soon to be added. Pedro had told BJ all about what had transpired that day and after. Cash had owned a club and a all female barbershop that was seized because it was in Blazes name. They also seized two houses and six vehicles from Blazes home. Because they weren't investigating Ms. Lopez's empire, everything they owned was still in good tact and soon to be passed on to BJ. Looking at the portrait of his parents made him smile. Pedro had always told him how his parents were so in love. He told BJ everything from the day Cash had first met Brooklyn up until the wedding. BJ often wondered if he would find love like his mom and dad. Even through the bullshit that they put each other through, their love was still genuine and real. Now that Aaliyah was in the picture he had a different outlook on the L word. As bad as he wanted to take the chance with Aaliyah, he also didn't want to be made a fool. Aaliyah was to damn fine and with her thot ass attitude he was sure she was fucking 90 going north.

"You still here Mijo?" Pedro asked walking into his room.

"Yeah. I decided to just stay home." BJ sighed looking up at the ceiling. Pedro was no dummy, he knew when something was on his son's mind.

"Its that chick from school huh?" Pedro asked causing BJ to laugh.

"How you know?"

"Because you got everything in the world a teenager could possibly have, And with that pitiful look, I'm more than sure its something with a woman."

"Yeah it's like I don't know what to do with her. I know I treat her bad but she a playa."

"And how do you know this?"

"I just do Papa. First off I already had to beat a nigga ass because of her. Then she act ratchet as hell and her best friend ain't no saint by far."

"Well Mijo you can't judge her based on what her friend does." Pedro said and turned to face BJ. "Ima tell you like this Papi, if you have to lay up in the bed and think about a chic, then you shouldn't waste your time thinking, you should be laid up with her. All those chicas you got and I've never seen you like this over one. She must be worth it." Pedro looked at BJ for agreement. When BJ shrugged his shoulders, Pedro continued. "I'm not gonna preach to you all night but I will say this. Don't miss out on a good thing because of your stubbornness. When my wife died, I hadn't dated for almost 20 years. Then I met Rosa. I gave that mujer a hard time. After years of Rosa trying, I had finally giving her a chance. The day your mother died is the day I regretted ever being a stubborn son of a bitch, because me and Rosa's love was short lived. Now I wish I could go back to the first day I had met her and give her a chance all over again." BJ looked at Pedro and he could tell this was a sore subject for him, however, he appreciated the guidance Pedro was blessing him with. He thought long and hard on what Pedro was saying, and it all made great sense. Though he wasn't sure that Aaliyah would be his Rosa, he would still give her a chance. For the remainder of the night BJ spent his friday with his Papa. they grabbed a few snacks and went into the den to watch movies. Thoughts of Aaliyah reigned heavy on his mind, so periodically he would stalk her instagram.

CHAPTER 5 *(Aaliyah)*

"If this is what love feels like, then I don't want it"

A few weeks had passed by and Aaliyah couldn't be more happy. BJ had been extremely nice to her and even went out of his way to make sure they talked on the phone daily. During school, they would walk each other to class and meetup to have lunch. It appeared as if love was in the air, because Venicia and Cali had been doing the same. Though, Cali wasn't trying to make Venicia his girl, she was content with the sex, dates and the every now and again phone calls. Aaliyah and BJ were taking things slow for the most part. Aaliyah had thought about asking BJ out but she didn't want to seem thirsty. BJ hadn't asked her to be his girlfriend and it was driving her crazy. She couldn't understand why because the way they talked and flirted had seemed as if they were more than friends anyway.

As Aaliyah pranced around her room, she prepared herself for a outing with Venicia. With so much begging and pleading, Mario had finally agreed to let her go. He had also mentioned that Ross would be Aaliyah's driver for the day as if Aaliyah would be upset. Little did Mario know, she couldn't be happier. Ross was pretty lenient with Aaliyah unlike Jeco who watched her every move and would also report her whereabouts.

Once she was done dressing, she went downstairs of the 90,000 square feet home in search of Ross. She was so excited and anxious to leave because she couldn't wait to see BJ. BJ and Cali had no clue the girls would be showing up tonight but she was sure he'd be just as excited. The Arcade is where all the kids in Miami hung out. It was located on the beach so after playing games and having fun, the young teens would always occupy themselves in the water. Aaliyah was more than sure Cali had talked BJ into coming because everyone from school and even residents would be there today.

Packing her bikini, sandals and her suntan lotion, Aaliyah was ready to hit the streets. She went outside where Ross had a Maybach awaiting her and greeted her as she stepped into his presence. Ross opened the door for Aaliyah then proceeded to his side to get in. Before entering the car, Ross made sure to adjust his 9 millimeter firearm and also checked his pockets for his two extra clips.

"Do you have to take that thing everywhere Ross?" Aaliyah asked annoyed. Aaliyah hated guns, and especially when she had to leave the house with one. Aaliyah wasn't a dummy. She understood her grandfather's life style but what she didn't understand was, what did it have to do with her.

"Yes Mija. you know its strict orders." Ross left it at that then pulled out of the driveway. Aaliyah sat back not trying to further the conversation, she was just happy to be out the house.

***

After picking up Venicia, it only took twenty minute for the girls to be pulling up to the Arcade. The entire ride they giggled and gossiped about the guys, but now Aaliyah had jitters. She was almost afraid to exit the vehicle but of course Venicia's bold ass would entice her. "Girl get outtt!" Venicia said adding emphasis. The two exit the car and made their way towards the arcade. Against his bosses order, Ross stayed in the car and let Aaliyah have fun. He made sure to keep a close eye on the girls but he would let them roam freely. Ross understood how life was as a teen because he also had kids himself. He loved Aaliyah like his own child and hated how Mario would treat the child, so he cut her a little slack.

When Aaliyah and Venicia walked into the arcade it was lit. Though it was a typical saturday night, Aaliyah's night would be more spectacular now that she had something to look forward too. With a slight appetite, the girls made their way to the back where the tables were to order some pizza. Stopping in her tracks, Aaliyah was instantly devastated. BJ sat at the table snickering in the face of some random chick. She was smiling while he laughed with her and Cali. When the guys looked up, they were just as shocked as the girls but they kept their composure intact. Aaliyah and BJ locked eyes and it was as if his eyes pleaded. Aaliyah could tell he was just as shocked as she was but it was much worse than that. With much anger and embarrassment, she walked over to an empty table down the aisle. As bad as she wanted to leave, she stayed because she didn't want to seem like a hater. Her and BJ weren't official but she couldn't help feel the pain inside.

"Don't sweat that shit Liyah." Venicia said looking at her best friend.

"I'm good Venicia. I promise I am."

"Good because you already know, fuck these niggas."

Yeah easy for you to say. Aaliyah thought to herself. *Cali ain't the one snickering in some bitch face so it's easier said than done.* She also thought but making sure to keep her comments to herself. Cali walked over to greet the girls as they looked thru the menus. He knew Aaliyah was pissed by the facial expression she wore and he actually felt bad for her. Since Cali had known Aaliyah, she was always sweet to him. Though he was once in love with her, and she'd always turned him down, she was still so sweet to him.

"Stop looking like that Liyah." Cali said taking a seat. "She aint nobody ma. Trust me if he knew you were coming, that bitch wouldn't even be here." Cali spoke truthfully. Since he and BJ had became closer, he got to meet Kamela and her hoeish ways. Cali could tell Kamela only wanted BJ because of his looks, swag and money so he didn't care for her company. She was only seventeen years old but that didn't stop anything. Kamela would bust it open for any nigga that had something to offer her stank ass. Because BJ was his boy, he choose to keep his antics to himself and let his patna do him.

"I'm good Cali." Aaliyah smiled weakly. Every now and then she would sneak a peek at BJ. She could tell he now felt bad because he slid slightly over and also kept stealing glances over at Aaliyah.

Kamela had looked over a few times wondering where was BJ's attention. When she noticed where he was looking, she instantly became upset. Being the petty bitch she was, she reached over and threw her arms around BJ's neck then planted trails of kisses down the side of his face. Trying her hardest to remain calm, Aaliyah couldn't take the sight before her. She jumped to her feet and stormed outside. Running as fast as she could, she passed up the car that awaited Ross and kept running towards the water. Her feelings were beyond hurt. BJ was her world and even though they weren't official, she couldn't fathom the thought of another woman having him. She fell to her knees and the tears she tried to hold back, came pouring down. As she looked out into the ocean the air felt nice against her skin. The sound of the ocean's waves crashing, slightly soothed her but she was heart broken. The tears slowly ran down her face and she was lost in her thoughts. Her phone ringing, knocked her out her thoughts but she didn't want to be bothered. She looked at the caller ID and it was Venicia. She sent the call to voicemail just as another call came through. It was Ross. she knew that Venicia had probably went to the car in search for her and that's why he was calling. She answered the phone trying to sound as if she was ok.

"Hey Ross, I'll be ready in a moment ok."

"Okay Mija. I'm waiting for you."

"Okay."

"Aaliyah?"

"Yes?"

"Are you ok?"

"Yes I'm fine. I'm just getting some air. I'm right on the beach I'll be over in a sec."

"Okay, I'm parked out front."

"Okay." were Aaliyah's last words as she disconnected the call. She sighed heavily, as she dropped her phone into her purse. *If this is what love feels like then I don't want it.* She thought to herself feeling defeated.

CHAPTER 6 *(Brooklyn Jr.)*

"Can you teach me how to love?"

The moment BJ and Aaliyah locked eyes, he cursed himself for bringing Kamela along. He had no idea Aaliyah would show up because Cali had confirmed how strict her parents were. BJ knew Aaliyah liked him but because she never made a move or insinuated being his girl, he figured she only liked him as a friend. Her jumping up from the table and storming out confirmed her feelings for him. Now he was upset because he knew Kamela had done that shit on purpose. He didn't like Kamela, he only loved her sex. For a seventeen year old, she was very experienced and could suck dick as if her life was depending on it. After today he was done with her petty behavior. He knew he had to console Aaliyah so he went into his pocket and pulled out a hundred dollar bill and handed it to Kamela telling her to go catch an uber home. At first she was trying to put up a fight but looking over the crisp hundred, her eyes lit up as she grabbed it. BJ shook his head at how money hungry she was and wondered what her mother was like. The vibration of his phone distracted his thoughts. He looked at his phone and ignored the call from a chic name Ameier. Instead he sent his Papa a text.

BJ: *You ain't gonna believe this shit Papa.*

Papa: *What happen Mijo you okay?*

BJ: *Yeah I'm straight. I'm with Kamela at the arcade and Aaliyah showed up.*

Papa: *Wow! So what you do?*

BJ: *I didn't know what to do. Aaliyah stormed out.*

Papa: *Well you gotta go find her Papi. That bitch Kamela means you no good. Vuelve a tu chica*!

BJ couldn't help but laugh at his Papa's text. Without replying, he slid his phone into his pocket and walked out to do as told.

BJ searched the parking lot and beach for Aaliyah until he found her. When he laid eyes on her, she was sitting in the sand looking out into the water. The radiant sun beaming down on Aaliyah's skin gave her a glow that made her more prettier. He stood back and watched her for a moment. He noticed that she was crying because periodically she would use the back of her hand to wipe her face and that shit killed him. BJ had never in his life felt pain like he was now feeling. Instead of making Aaliyah smile he was the one causing her pain. At this very moment he knew he had to make it up to her so he would step up to the plate and make things official.

"It ain't even like that baby girl." BJ said placing his hand on Aaliyah's shoulder. She looked up to BJ but didn't say a word. She dropped her head and a lone tear slid down her right cheek. She quickly wiped it away, but it was too late, BJ had already knew she had been crying. Aaliyah you hear me talking ma?"

"Brooklyn please just leave me alone." She shot causing BJ to slightly smile. He loved the way Aaliyah called him by his first name.

"I'm not leaving until you talk to me."

"There's nothing to talk about."

"It's a lot to talk about. Like why you tripping and you ain't my girl."

"I'm not tripping BJ. I don't want you" "You wanna be my girl Ma?" BJ asked ignoring her smart remark. "Huh? Answer me. You wanna be my girl Liyah? Don't lie please don't lie." He said burning a hole in her face. Finally Aaliyah looked up at him with so much hurt in her eyes. She had slightly shook her head and that blew BJ back. He took a seat besides her and looked out into the ocean. He was trying his hardest to gather his thoughts before speaking because he didn't want to say the wrong things.

"I've never been in love before so this shit hard for me. Ima be honest ma, since the first day I saw you at school a nigga was instantly drawn to you. I know you're worth every ounce of my love I just don't want to break yo heart. All my life, I been a loner. No family, no friends, shit all I do is fuck bitches and chill with ma Papa. I don't even know how to love Liyah. Can you teach me how to love? Because I promise if you teach me how to love, I'll love you till my dying days." Aaliyah was blown back by every word. Though it hurt her to know the real him, she loved the fact that he was truthful. She looked him in the eyes and right then and there she saw what most people didn't see. Looking at BJ you would think he was a spoiled ass d-boy but to Aaliyah she saw much more. She saw a broken kid, a good heart and savage wrapped into one person. She didn't know the story behind his life but she knew that he was tormented from his past.

"Can you do that for me ma?" BJ asked knocking Aaliyah from her thoughts. Her insides were smiling and she wanted to jump into his arms. Instead she nodded her head yes. The slight smile she displayed made BJ feel a lot better. He was now happy he could turn her frown into a smile. He pulled her into his arms and kissed the top of her forehead. He didn't know shit about love but for Aaliyah he would give it a try.

"Where are your parents Brooklyn?" Aaliyah asked the question she had been wondering for some time. Talking about his parents was a soft subject for BJ. The only person he talked to about the explosion was his Papa. Since things had changed for the two teens, BJ decided to open up to his future wife.

"They died the day of their wedding."

"Oh my god, I'm sorry to hear that BJ. What happened? If you don't mind me asking."

"Nah you good baby. The Yacht they hosted their wedding on blew up killing everyone aboard. My mother, my father, my grandma and my parents friends. I'm talking bestfriends, kids everybody. I lost a little brother and all." BJ dropped his head. When he looked up, Aaliyah had tears streaming down her face. He studied her long and hard and right then and there he knew; Aaliyah loved him sincerely.

"Don't cry baby." He pulled her closer into his arms. BJ looked around the beach and had nearly forgotten where they were. It was a nice evening and people were everywhere. The sun had gone down but it was still a bit warm out.

"I'm sorry bae. I just get emotional because I'm in the same boat. My mother was killed when I was a few months old so I never got a chance to know her. I don't know where my father is. I live with my grandfather and his staff. I always ask about my father but for some reason, my grandpa don't like when I ask him questions." BJ's eyes bucked at the information. He knew right then Aaliyah was his soul mate. He would never have thought in his life that

Aaliyah suffered the same pain from losing the most important people in the world.

"So do you wanna find him?" BJ asked.

"I mean yeah but my grandpa would kill me." She looked out into the sky.

"Shit what if he don't know?" BJ smirked looking at his princess.

"You'll help me Brooklyn?" Aaliyah smiled widely. When he shook his head yes, she jumped to her knees and hugged him tightly.

"Aaliyah Vamonos Mija." Ross walked up causing the two to jump. BJ stood to his feet and eyed Ross unsure as to who he was. Aaliyah also stood to her feet but unlike BJ, she wore a look of fear. Even though Ross was lenient with Liyah, she didn't know how he would react knowing she had a boyfriend. She prayed he wouldn't tell her grandfather.

"I have to go BJ." Aaliyah spoke sadly because her night was now coming to an end.

"Its cool baby girl. I'll see you monday at school."

"Where's Cali?" she asked

"He left with Venicia."

"So how you gonna get home?"

"Shit I don't know. My whip at home I rode with Cali. But I'm good Ma, I'll call my Papa or just catch an uber." Aaliyah looked over at Ross with pleading eyes. Ross knew he could not only lose his job but he would also lose his life, but he couldn't bring himself to tell Aaliyah no.

"Vamonos." He looked at Aaliyah and BJ. Aaliyah smiled and grabbed BJ's hand leading him towards the car.

Inside the car Aaliyah and BJ talked about everything under the sun. He was happy he took the next step with her because she was a cool female. He loved everything about her. He had learned that she was Cuban and she was also happy to find out he was Puerto Rican. The two knew spanish all though they hated speaking it, they were so intrigued at how many things they had in common. The entire ride home, they held hands and were lost in their conversations. BJ felt awkwardly weird because he had never done this before, but he wouldn't trade the feeling in for the world.

Pulling up to BJ's beach house, he hated that their night had to end. He really enjoyed himself with his new girl and couldn't wait to see her again. Ross granted them permission to exit the car and exchange good byes. BJ kissed her on the lips but nothing to extreme because he didn't want Ross to feel disrespected. He held her door open to help her back in the car. Once the car was out of sight BJ jogged up to his front door, and Pedro already awaited him. The door swung open and Pedro stood smiling.

"What old man?" BJ grinned at his Papa.

"I take it, you guys made up?" Pedro smiled with a raised eyebrow.

"Yeah that was her. We made it official." BJ smiled. Pedro patted his child on the back and told him "good job." Before BJ walked off Pedro called out to him.

"Papi!" BJ turned around. "What does her parents do?"

"Shit I don't know. Well her mom died when she was a baby and her pops just disappeared."

"Oh okay. I was just asking because the only people that drive those fancy carros are either drug dealers or the president." Pedro spoke truthfully. Pedro began to cough loudly causing BJ to rush over to him. Pedro then waved BJ off to let him know he was okay. Watching Pedro closely, BJ made his way to his room. He told himself over and over that he would not go to sleep until his Papa was sleeping peacefully.

CHAPTER 7 *(Aaliyah)*

"Yes, I Love You"

Over the course of a month, BJ and Aaliyah had been inseparable. They would meet up first thing in the morning for school, they held hands as they walked through the hallways and they would even meet up on weekends. Things were different because they were now an item. Mario had been out of town twice, something he did regularly so that gave Aaliyah the freedom she needed to be with her man. All though BJ wasn't allowed to come to visit Aaliyah's home, she was grateful that Pedro was different. She was always at BJ's home. She had finally met Pedro and from the first day she fell in love with him. He was a very generous man and she loved the bond him and BJ shared. Most days she would watch how the two interacted, and she would wish she had that same bond with her own grandfather. Even though Mario gave Aaliyah everything she desired, she still hated how he was always gone and how he would keep her held like a prisoner. He never spent time with the young teen. He felt that if he had giving Liyah the world, she would be content. But to Aaliyah, money wasn't the key to her happiness, she wanted to feel loved like most kids. Aaliyah couldn't lie, BJ and Pedro filled the void that her grandfather had left. She enjoyed being over BJ's. They would talk amongst the three and most nights Pedro would cook up a hearty meal. Many times she had fallen asleep in his arms and not once had he tried to make a move on her. She knew that sooner or later it would happen so she gave herself the pep talk she needed. Deep down inside, Aaliyah knew BJ was the one she wanted to give her mind, body and soul. She wanted him and only him, and she wanted him to have all of her as well.

The sound of BJ’s phone knocked Aaliyah's thoughts back from her mind. She lifted off of his bed and went to the dresser to take a peek at its blinking screen. She smirked when she saw Kamela's name appear across the screen but she wouldn't dare open the message. Aaliyah picked up the phone then headed out the room towards the restroom. Passing by Pedro’s room she heard him coughing something terribly. She pushed the door open and ran to his side.

“Papa you ok?” she asked calling Pedro by the name he had told her to call him.

“I'm fine Mija. I just need some agua.” Aaliyah quickly ran out of the room to the kitchen. She grabbed the bottled water from the fridge and ran back towards the room but bumping into BJ.

“Whats wrong ma?” BJ asked looking at Aaliyah who wore a panicked look.

“Its Papa. he’s really sick.”

“I know but he always says he's fine.”

“I'm gonna give him his water. Oh and your boo is calling you.” Aaliyah smirked and handed BJ his cell. She went back into the room and handed Pedro the water. She then went over to his dresser and retrieved his medicine. Opening the top she handed him the yellow pill and stood still until he took it.

“Thanks Liyah.” Pedro smiled weakly.

“Your welcome Papa.” she smiled back then exited the room.

It was something about Aaliyah that Pedro took a liking too. He knew that Aaliyah was the perfect girl for BJ, however he prayed the young boy would do right by her. BJ still had lots of growing up to do, so he knew that he would cause Aaliyah some sort of pain in their young relationship. Aaliyah reminded Pedro of Cash when she was a young girl. Everything from her beauty to her innocence. Aaliyah was a smart girl and Pedro loved how she would come over and get straight to her books. Because of BJ's wild side, he was sure that Aaliyah would be BJ's calm. Since the two had been together, Pedro saw a major change in BJ. The many women that BJ kept in his company had now vanished. All he talked about was Aaliyah and if she wasn't in their home, they would be on the phone until the wee hours of the night.

Walking into BJ's room, Aaliyah looked on as BJ had the cell phone nestled to his ear and shoulder. He was sliding into some gym shorts but not once looking up at Aaliyah. She could tell he was on the phone with a chick by the way he was answering the questions. Every word was short, "nah, yeah, aight" was all she heard. She took a seat on the bed and began browsing through her phone.

"I'm with my girl so I'll call you back." BJ spoke then looked over at Aaliyah.

"Matter of fact, just lose my number." He told the caller and hung up. Aaliyah acted as if she was unfazed by BJ's phone call but in fact she was smiling inside. She was happy he had dismissed the caller, however, she knew that it wouldn't be the last time she called back.

Aaliyah stood to her feet and began kissing BJ intensely. She loved everything about BJ from his thug demor to the tattoos that covered his body. Just looking at him shirtless made her kitty jump in her jeans. She craved BJ's touch but she wasn't ready to give herself to him. She knew deep down BJ would be the one to take her virginity, but she wanted to wait until the right time.

The two stood in the middle of BJ's room making out. Their hands roamed each others body and the heat between them began to burn wider. Aaliyah had never told BJ she was a virgin because she didn't want him to look at her like a little girl. In BJ's mind Aaliyah had slept with several guys and figured she just wasn't ready.

"You betta stop girl before I bend that ass over." BJ smirked. Aaliyah only laughed and brushed the comment off.

"What you gonna do for your birthday?" Aaliyah asked changing the subject.

"Shit I don't know. Prolly spend it with my Papa."

"So you don't wanna go out?"

"I don't know, I mean if you wanna go out I'll take you but I'm not tripping. Cali tryna get me to go out with him but I keep telling that nigga no."

"Is that so? And where is this?"

"Some club called Exclusive."

"Oh. well maybe you should go. I mean you are about to be eighteen Brooklyn. Get out, have some fun baby."

"I'll think about it." BJ said and looked into space. BJ wasn't really into the whole club thing so going out he would have to give it much thought.

"What time you gotta go ma?" He asked Aaliyah reaching for the remote.

"I'll call Ross about eleven."

"When your grandpa coming back?"

"I don't know. He's always gone for weeks at a time."

"So why don't you just spend the night?"

"Because of the other guards. Everyone is so mean to me and I'm sure someone would tell." BJ's jaw clenched at the mention everyone is so mean to her. In his eyes Aaliyah was a sweet person.

"Man what is it your grandfather does? That nigga doing good for himself. Shit I see your pics of your crib on instagram, shit looks fly." BJ fished for information because he remembered what Pedro had said. Aaliyah began to fidget at the mention of her grandfather's lifestyle. She didn't know what to say, but she also didn't want to lie.

"He owns a few businesses and has money invested into lots of stocks." Aaliyah answered quickly and looked away. She didn't want to hold any secrets with BJ but she also didn't want him judging her by what her grandfather did for a living.

Plenty of times Aaliyah had heard conversations of him talking to his buyers. After putting two and two together, she figured he was the supplier for the entire state of Miami. She had also heard him ordering hits on people and that was the part she hated most. Aaliyah was a sweet innocent girl. The fact that her grandpa killing innocent people toyed with her feelings. She hated death, she hated guns and she also hated drugs. She vowed to herself that she would further her education and one day open her own business. She dreaded the day she could leave her grandfather's home and live off on her own.

"Can I ask you something?" BJ asked bringing her from her thoughts.

"Yes."

“Do you love me?”

“Yes I love you.” she spoke honestly. She knew that she was moving too fast, but she also couldn't help her feelings. She loved BJ with all of her heart, but the question was did he love her back. BJ nodded his head up and down but not once saying the words that she anticipated hearing. She took it as he didn't love her and it pained her inside. She picked up her phone and began scrolling through her instagram. BJ snatched her phone out of her hand and they began to wrestle for it. He quickly snapped a pic of them two together and uploaded it to Aaliyah's instagram. She jumped up and walked over to the charger where BJ’s phone was and slide it opened. She went to his instagram and did the same thing. After minutes of reading comments, she snuggled up under BJ and snapped another pic of them. She handed it to BJ so he could write a caption and post it. She was smiling widely exposing her dimples causing BJ to laugh. She picked up her phone and went to BJ’s page and she couldn't help but smile at his caption. *I belong to her!* Though BJ didn't tell Aaliyah he loved her, the caption made her feel much better. Because she still had a few hours to spare they snuggled up closely on the bed and began searching for a movie. A few minutes later, Aaliyah jumped for joy at the movie he had choose. She smirked at him because he knew it was her favorite, but what really made her blush was the fact that he had remembered. *Romeo Must Die*.

CHAPTER 8 *(Brooklyn Jr.)*

"Birthday Behavior"

The week had passed by quickly. Today was BJ's 18th birthday and he didn't really have any plans. It was saturday morning and he was tired as hell from talking to Aaliyah all night on the phone. She had wished him happy birthday a million and one times, and even posted him on her page twice. He was more than happy with the love he was getting from Cali and his many jumpoffs. Cali had been texting him all day to go out to the club. He was giving it some thought but for now he would spend the day with his Papa and girlfriend.

BJ got up and headed into the restroom to handle his morning hygiene. Passing by the living room, he had to do a double take. There was a table spread with all of BJ's favorite foods. He had lobster, crab legs, crawfish and red potatoes, corn on the cob and much more. No matter what time of the day, BJ ate his seafood with pride. He walked over to the table and picked up a crawfish. After scarfing down the crawfish he ran into the restroom and began his routine. Once he was done, he walked back out in search of his papa. Just when he was about to call out to his Papa, he walked through the front door holding a dozen balloons.

"Happy Birthday son!" Pedro smiled and pulled BJ in for a hug.

"Thanks Papa. Man this shit lookin good." BJ rubbed his hands together.

“I got something for you. Slide on your shoes and meet me outside. After this we could eat something Mijo.”

“Fasho.” BJ smiled and ran into his room. He slipped on his Nike slides then made his way out the door.

The morning air felt good to BJ the moment he stepped off the porch. The waves were crashing and the birds that flew over head gave him a peace of serenity. Pedro wasn't on the front porch so BJ went around to the back. When he made it out back his Papa was sitting in his ride. BJ opened the door and hopped in. Pedro pulled out of the garage and headed where BJ had no clue. After a few moments of driving they pulled up to the doc that was privately owned. Pedro exited the car and told BJ to follow him. BJ stepped out the car unsure of what awaited ahead. He followed Pedro closely and stopped in front of a 2017 Horizon E75 yacht. It was baby blue with two white stripes. On the side of it in big bold letters it read ‘*Papi*’ in cursive writing. BJ looked from Pedro to the yacht then back to Pedro. He was so ecstatic about the gift that he couldn't speak one word.

“Thanks Papa.” BJ smiled widely and gave Pedro a tight hug. This was the best gift he could ever receive.

“It's all yours my boy.” Pedro boosted happily.

“Man this the best gift ever!” BJ said almost in tears.

“Don't worry there’s more.” Pedro said and smiled again. “Hop on check it out.” Pedro told BJ. BJ walked on the the yacht and began examining it. It was equipped with a full-beam Master bedroom, a guest stateroom that can be converted to a double bed. The interior was fresh but elegant. It had a huge area for a party, two restrooms, and one that had a hot tub. There was also a kitchen and a built in bar. It was a double deck yacht that would take the breath of anybody that stepped foot on it. Pedro had out done himself spending nearly five million dollars for his boy.

After fooling around on the yacht for some time, Pedro insisted they go in the house and get ready to chow down. Leaving the yacht, BJ couldn't stop smiling. In his head, he already had plans for the boat. Walking back into their home, they headed straight for the table. They grabbed two of the china plates and began feasting.

"What you gonna do tonight Mijo?"

"I don't know. Cali want me to go out with him."

"You should go. Enjoy your self Papi. You're not getting any younger Mijo so live a little." Pedro said and stuffed a piece of lobster into his mouth. BJ was giving what Pedro said some thought. This was the second person that had told him the same thing in so many words so he made his mind up; he was going.

"Yeah Ima go. I gotta see what's up with Aaliyah though."

***

In his room BJ was getting ready to get his night started. After spending the entire day with his Papa, he was happy and now he would go off with his friend. He jumped into the shower and let the hot water massage his body but making sure not to wet his locks. After rinsing his body, he lathered his towel with his Irish Spring body wash that was his favorite. After soaping up, he rinsed off and stepped out the shower wrapping himself with his huge Jordan towel. When he made it into his room, his cell phone was blinking he had a message. He quickly dried off then picked it up. It was a message from Aaliyah that read.

Stinka: hey baby. My grandpa is back and he's tripping about me leaving. I'm really trying to come over.

Mi Papi: it's cool baby. Ima go fuck with Cali tonight. If you could get out hit me up so I could come get you.

Stinka: ok and you better behave while you with Cali ratchet ass. (smirk face)

Mi Papi: nah ma. I'm good. You the only woman I need Stinka

After BJ was done getting dressed he went into his Papa's study to let him know he was leaving. When he opened the door, his Papa sat behind his huge marble desk going through some paperwork. He removed his glasses the moment they made eye contact. It was something about the way his Papa looked at that made an electric volt rush through his body. They eyed each other for a moment and neither one spoke. Pedro lifted up a huge envelope and handed it to BJ breaking their stair down. For some odd reason BJ was a bit nervous. The look his Papa was giving him, let him know that the envelope contained something serious.

"Don't open it now Mijo. I want you to enjoy your night. Its nothing bad so you don't have to look like that but it's very serious information. Your a smart boy so I'm not worried one bit. I know you'll do good with this information and make the right choices.

"I'll get it when I come home tonight. cool?"

"Okay. I love you and have fun"

"I love you too Papa." BJ looked at Pedro "And thank you for everything." BJ spoke sincerely. Not only was he thanking his Papa for the best bday ever, he was also thanking him for his life. Pedro was the only important person in BJ's life. As hard core as the young boy was, the only person that could break him down was his Papa. The two shared a bond like a mother and child because they were all each other had. Now that Aaliyah was in BJ's life, he felt happy and complete. However, he knew women came a dime a dozen but his Papa wasn't replaceable.

Knowing he'd be drinking tonight, BJ decided to have Manuel drive him around town in his Papa's Rolls Royce. First he would pick up Cali, then they would hit the club. He was a bit disappointed he couldn't see his girl, but he would make the best of his night. He was looking good in a pair of Balmain Jeans, a brown Louis Vuitton V-neck Tee and a pair of Louis Vuitton sneakers. His locks were pulled back in a rubber band exposing his 5 karat platinum diamond studs. He kept it simple with his cuban link and bracelet to match. Little did Cali know, they would be shutting the club down. Because he was only 18 he couldn't be underestimated. He had plenty money to blow and he would be doing it in the VIP.

CHAPTER 9 *(Aaliyah)*

"I wanna umm..ummm.. Tonight."

Aaliyah sat in her room distort. Her grandfather was acting like the asshole he always acted like so she was stuck as the prisoner she was. She had been contemplating sneaking out but she thought against it. With the many guards that lingered around the mansion she knew she wouldn't make it out. The only way she could possibly get out the house was Venicia's mother. Aaliyah knew that if she asked, Mario would consider. She was the only person that Mario was slightly submissive too because Venicia and Aaliyah had been friends for some time. Venicia lived in a upscale part of town and her mother worked as an Elementary school teacher for over twenty years. Ms Campbell was a go getter and a true diva. On many occasions, Mario purposely dropped Aaliyah off himself so he could flirt with the woman. Because Mario was now divorced, he entertained plenty women on several occasions. Mario was a bit old, but he was still handsome for his age. His Cuban inheritance, gave him a peanut butter skin tone that most people would consider him to be an indian. His salt and pepper hair added to his looks, and the expensive suits he wore drove the women crazy. Aaliyah always saw how women would throw themselves at her grandfather but he was so powerful he rarely entertained them. Mario loved his woman from across the board and seasoned. For some odd reason he was attracted to Ms. Campbell and tonight Aaliyah would use it to her advantage. She picked up the phone and dialed her best friend.

"So what he say?" Venicia answered on the first ring.

"He still saying no. Man ask yo mom please" Aaliyah begged.

"Okay she just walked in. Ima ask her then hit you back."

"Okay hoe don't be havin me waiting all damn night."

"You think you slick huh. You tryna go to that damn club. Venicia laughed.

"Ugh no, I'm just trying get out this house."

"Girl boo. Im tryna go just as bad as you. I wanna spy on Cali hoe ass."

"Girl you too much." Aaliyah laughed at her BFF. Hanging up the phone, Aaliyah would wait patiently for her friend. She began scrolling through her gram so she could check on BJ's page. It was a picture of him and Cali in the backseat of a car. They both were looking debonair as they held up two bottles of "Ace of Spades" owned by the famous rapper Jay Z. Under the picture were many comments, mostly from women and a few guys from school wishing BJ a happy birthday. Aaliyah instantly got jealous like she had been doing all day. She knew inside that club that there would be many women flaunting their asses around her man so she wanted badly to be in attendance. Aaliyah wasn't threatened by any woman on earth, because she knew she was beautiful. She knew her man would shut the club down with his looks and swag, and she too would be turning heads upon entrance. Aaliyah began to pack her bags, because she knew that Mario would agree to Ms. Campbell asking for her permission.

***

The club was in full swing. Thanks to Venicia knowing the bouncers, they were let in without a problem. Aaliyah was a bit nervous but she held her chin up and put on her big girl panties.

They walked inside and went straight to the bar. Venicia was a drinker at such young age, however, Aaliyah would settle for a glass of Moet dry. On their way to the bar, they were stopped by many men who appeared to be already tipsy. The ladies were looking good and all eyes were on them. Venicia was wearing a two piece crop top and pencil skirt with matching pumps. Her hair was in a updo with bangs and her makeup was light and simple. Aaliyah on the other hand was rocking a tan bodycon dress that fell of the shoulders. It was simple but sexy. Her cruel summer heels adorned her feet and she rocked a gold clutch to match her gold body chain. Her hair was bone straight with a bang covering one eye giving her a look like the singer Aaliyah. It had a slight feather to it that she would constantly push out of her face. Her makeup was applied lightly making her appear much older than what she was. Now this was a side of her that BJ had never seen. She dressed cute at school but she only wore wedge heels and jeans mainly. Tonight she was looking grown, feeling sexy, and there was only one man in the entire club that she wanted.

"Look at these niggas." Venicia said looking onto the upper level of the club. Aaliyah's eyes followed the direction she was looking and her eyes landed right on BJ's. They instantly locked eyes and held each other's gaze. BJ blinked his eyes several times, as if he didn't believe it was her. With one finger he motioned for her to come to him. Aaliyah blushed shyly then gave Venicia a slight elbow push. She stood to her feet and pulled her friend closely behind her. With the sexist walk she could muster up, Aaliyah strutted to BJ's VIP with much confidence.

The moment the girls reached the section, BJ pulled Aaliyah in and hugged her then placed a gentle kiss on her neck. Aaliyah who was shy like, snickered into the nape of his neck slightly embarrassed. She could smell the alcohol that seeped from BJ's pours and she knew right then he was a bit intoxicated. He broke the hug, then stepped back to look over Aaliyah's attire. The rubbing hands together, and the way he licked his lips let Aaliyah know that he liked what he saw. *Perfect.* She thought to herself smiling at her boo seductively. Tonight she had planned on giving herself to BJ but she didn't know how to go about it.

When Aaliyah looked over, Cali and Venicia were snuggled up closely on the two seater white leather sofa. "Damn hi Cali!" Aaliyah shouted causing Cali and Venicia to look up. They both wore enormous smiles that made everyone laugh. Cali stood to his feet and gave Aaliyah a hug. He complimented her look then walked off to where Venicia awaited.

"You lookin hella good Stinka."

"Thank you Mi Papi. You looking good too." Aaliyah spoke shly.

"Why yo ass always being shy ma? Daddy make you scared?" BJ said looking Aaliyah in her eyes. He grabbed her face softly with both hands. *Damn this boy is sexy.* She thought to herself.

"Brooklyn?" Aaliyah called out to BJ just above a whisper.

"Yeah ma."

"I wanna umm… ummm.. Tonight." Aaliyah stumbled over every word.

"Word. you sure you ready for that?" BJ replied already knowing what she was getting at. Aaliyah nodded her head yes then dropped her head. BJ's quietness only made her more nervous. When she looked up he was looking her square dead in the face, but she could tell his thoughts were in a whole other place.

"Aye BJ I got somebody I want you to meet." Cali said walking over knocking the two lovebirds from their thoughts.

Aaliyah walked over and took a seat on the sofa with Venicia so they could give the guys some privacy. Everything Venicia started babbling about only went in one ear and out the other. Aaliyah's attention was fixated on her boo. Every woman that walked by the VIP and laid eyes on BJ were mesmerized. Aaliyah couldn't be mad because she knew she had the flyest young nigga in the club. What really made her smile, was the fact that BJ paid the girls no attention. Every chance he had gotten to look away, he would steal glances at his girl. The way he looked at her, was as if they were the only two in the room. Their eyes held so much passion and fire, Aaliyah knew that tonight would be the night. *Sheesh.*

CHAPTER 10 *(Brooklyn Jr.)*

"Papa Nooo! Please don't leave me!"

"Whats up youngin happy Bday." Cali's brother had said to BJ. He shook his hand and gave Young a manly hug then stepped back to take a swig from his bottle.

"Good looking Young."

"Man this how yo little ass doing it?" Young asked looking around the VIP then glancing in the direction of Aaliyah and Venicia. Don't get it twisted, Young was rolling in dough. However, he knew BJ was young so that puzzled him as to what he did for a living. He knew that either BJ sold coke or his parents had to be doctors or lawyers. Cali had told Young a lot about BJ and also told him how BJ and his Papa lived. The one thing Cali left out was how BJ's Papa got dough because Cali was clueless. BJ was a smart young man and no matter how close the two became, it wasn't anyone's business. Straight up. BJ had knew all about how his Papa made money in his past life. Pedro had made so much money working for the empire and many other Cartels, that he was able to retire and live well off as a billionair.

Young stood back and closely watched BJ. It was something about the young boy that appeared very familiar. He couldn't put his finger on it, but he would sure pry to find out.

"Brooklyn." Aaliyah called out to BJ. Young's face squinched at the name but quickly shook the thought off. He watched BJ as he walked over to the pretty light bright girl who had called his name.

"Whats up ma?" BJ slurred as he walked over to Aaliyah.

"Can you pour me a glass of champagne?"

"Yo little ass drinking tonight?" BJ laughed. He walked over to the table and began pouring Aaliyah's drink. For some reason he felt odd about the way Young was watching him. *I hope I ain't gotta body this nigga.* BJ thought to himself ignoring Young's gaze. After he poured her cup, he walked back over and asked if she was ready to bounce. BJ had had enough of the club scene and he was ready to get knee deep in his princesses pussy.

After the four agreed that Cali would be riding home with Venicia, Aaliyah and BJ walked out the establishment hand and hand. When they made it to the car, BJ instructed Manuel to take them to the Ritz Carlton Hotel. BJ looked over at Aaliyah who looked a bit nervous. He pulled her close to him to lighten the mood. He didn't understand why she was such a wreck because he was sure she had been fucked numerous of times. He waved it off as it being their first time together.

When they made it inside the hotel, BJ headed for the shower. Aaliyah took a seat on the bed and began fidgeting. She picked up the remote and began flicking threw the movies that the hotel had. She was a bit tipsy but not enough that she couldn't function properly. Dropping the remote, Aaliyah mustard up enough courage to walk into the restroom. When she opened the door, BJ had his back to her. The water running down BJ's many tattoos was a sight to see. Watching BJ through the glass doors made her love box jump between her legs. BJ turned around and nearly jumped out of his skin.

"Damn girl you scared me. Why you creeping up on a nigga?" He laughed. Aaliyah remained quiet because she had gotten the shock of her lifetime. BJ's erect dick was bulging. She couldn't believe her eyes. She never thought that such a young man could have been so blessed. BJ looked her in the eyes hungrily, and began stroking himself seductively. BJ wasn't a ameture when it came to pleasing a woman. He had been with many chicks and even much older than him. Noticing that Aaliyah wasn't hopping in to join him, he climbed out and began drying himself off. Aaliyah walked out of the restroom embarrassed and laid back down on the bed. BJ walked out into the room, and looked over Aaliyah who was still fully dressed.

"You sure you wanna do this ma?" He asked her unsure.

"Yes." Was all she said.

"Well take that shit off." He spoke walking closer to the bed.

Aaliyah slowly pealed out of her dress and even removing her panty and bra set. BJ watched her in awe. This was his first time seeing her completely naked and damn she looked good. Her body was blemish free and perfect. She had a nice size set of tits and her ass sat up as if she had gotten a few injections. BJ licked his lips and nodded his head in agreeance. He positioned himself on top of her and began placing soft kisses down her neck. He wasn't into much foreplay but because Aaliyah belonged to him he was willing. He moved down to her love box and spread her legs. He looked at it closely as if it would talk back to him. With his tongue he began to flicker it across her pearl tongue. With just one taste, it was like licking a lollipop. She taste so good to him, he began to devour her. With every lick, he could feel her body tense up. "Relax ma." He told her but it was easier said than done.

After making Aaliyah have her first organsim ever, BJ was ready to pulverise her pretty pussy. She was breathing heavy like she was done, but little did she know the rollercoaster ride had just began. He lifted her legs apart, holding the heel of her foot in the palm of his hands. He positioned himself at her opening. With one hand he used the tip of his dick to massage her clit. Because she was already dripping wet, he knew that it would be much easier inserting himself. “Oooh” Aaliyah let out a sexy moan that drove BJ crazy. He put the tip of his manhood into Aaliyah’s opening, and tried to force its way in. Aaliyah's moans turned into a cry like whimper as he pushed himself inside deeper. “Got damn.” BJ growled. Her pussy was tighter than he expected. Not even a minute inside of her he was precumming pre-maturely.

“Oh my god BJ, its to big baby. It hurts.” She cried out.

“You want me to stop?”

“No don't stop. Ohh don't stop.” Aaliyah continued to cry out. After a few more strokes the pain had finally eased up and she was ready for the full him.

BJ was hitting her with long nice strokes that had her eyes rolling in the back of her head. The kisses he was placing all over body as he stroked her, made her feel like the girls in the romantic movies. He wasn't fucking her, he was making love to her.

“I love you Stinka.” He spoke the words right when she was thinking it.

“I love you too Papito.” She said with so much passion. After tonight, things would be different with BJ and his Princess. They had done the one last thing that could possibly make them closer. There was no turning back and neither of the two seemed to care.

***

The next morning BJ walked into the door of him and his Papa's beach house. He was so happy that his birthday turned out the best, he couldn't wait to fill his Papa in on his night. He was gonna tell him everything even up until the morning when him and Aaliyah departed ways. BJ and his Papa had a great bond so he was gonna tell him how bomb Aaliyah's pussy was. He couldn't help but laugh to himself as he walked into his Papa's room. His Papa was laying in the bed asleep. It was strange because Pedro would move at the slightest noise. BJ figured he was tired but he wanted let him know he had made it home safe and sound.

"Papa." BJ called out walking closer to the bed. "Papa." He called out again but this time shaking Pedro lightly. *Damn he must be tired.* BJ thought as he shook him harder. When Pedro didn't budge, the last aggressive shake BJ began to panic. He touched Pedros head and it was freezing cold. Shaking Pedro over and over BJ began to cry. "Papa wake up. Im home." BJ cried out, but his Papa wouldn't move. BJ pulled out his phone and shot Manuel a text letting him know to hurry over. He ran back to his Papa's bedside in hopes he would wake up and the reality finally set in, his Papa had passed in his sleep. "Papa Nooo, Please don't leave me!" BJ cried harder. He cried so hard he fell to the floor devastated. The pain he felt was something unreal. BJ had never endured such terrible pain. His Papa was all he had and at this point he felt like he didn't want to go on living. His mother was gone, his father was gone, his abuelita was gone and now the only person in the world he loved; was gone.

CHAPTER 11 *(Aaliyah)*

"I'm not into chasin' no nigga. I'm too fly for that."

It had been a week since Aaliyah last spoken to BJ. she was beyond hurt. She felt played, she felt pain, and most of all she felt like a complete fool. She had called and texted him numerous of times but every call went unanswered. He hadn't been to school and even Cali said he hadn't saw nor heard from his boy since the night of the club. Aaliyah sat in her room daily and cried herself to sleep. Over and over she had told herself that she was through with love because again she had been burned. At first she was worried about BJ but then she figured he had gotten what he wanted and just moved on. She felt like such a fool because she had giving him her most valuable possession. She thought everything about the night was magical. When he told her he loved her, she believed him because it seemed so sincere. She wanted to go by his house badly but she thought against it not wanting to seem thirsty. The sound of her door opening made her look up from her bed. Through the bed curtains she could see the figure of her grandpa entering the room. She rolled back over to her side, turning her back to him. The sound of his footsteps let Aaliyah know he had walked further into her room. He took a seat on the bed and Aaliyah could feel his eyes burning a hole threw her.

"Mija are you ok?" Mario asked.

"I'm fine Apa." she lied.

"Well you haven't been out of this room. And Blanca told me you haven't been really eating."

"I just been feeling a little sick. I think I'm catching the flu." Again she lied.

"You sure it's the flu?" Mario questioned with one eye bra raised. "You sure it's not some pendejo got you lookin all sad and shit." He spoke with much base. Aaliyah remained quiet only drawing up his suspicions. "Aaliyah, I know you're getting older and you're becoming curious. But you have to remain focused Mija. These guys mean you no good."

"It's not a boy Apa. I just been feeling under the weather." She smiled weakly. Mario was no fool, he read between the lines and prayed that his grandchild would come to her senses.

"Okay Mija, I have something for you. Put your clothes on and come outside."

"Okay." she nodded her head. Mario lifted off her bed and headed out the door.

Aaliyah really didn't want to be bothered with her grandfather but she wouldn't dare ignore his orders to come outside. She lifted off the bed and slid her feet into her pink Puma slides. She made her way down the long spiral staircase and went out the door. The first person she spotted was Blanca. She had a slight smile on her face that made Aaliyah wonder what was going on.

"Hey Blanca."

"Hey Mija. your apa is waiting for you by the courts." Blanca told her. Aaliyah hopped on the golf cart that was used to drive her around the home. Because the mansion was huge, the courts were on the other side of the yard.

Driving up to the court, Aaliyah stopped the cart in front of her Apa who was smiling widely. She couldn't help but laugh at his goofy grin. Mario was always uptight but when he was in a great mood he was mad cool. Aaliyah looked in the direction that her Apa looked into and the moment her eyes landed on the 2018 drop top Mercedes Benz E-class Aaliyah's eyes beamed with hearts sorta like her favorite emoji. She ran into the arms of her Apa and hugged him tightly. She was beyond happy until reality sat in that she wouldn't be able to drive the car because of how strict he was.

"Thank you." she smiled hesitantly.

"Don't look like that Aaliyah you could drive it Mija. There will be certain rules and sometimes I will send detail behind you. But for the most part I'll ease up a bit." Aaliyah smiled at her grandpa's words. *What done got into him?* She eyed him suspiciously with a slight smile. Her phone began to vibrate in her hands and she looked down.

Ms. Campbell: *so I take it you love your gift*

Was what the text read. Aaliyah giggled because she should have known. Her fingers began to move swiftly as she grinned but responded to her text.

Aaliyah: *yess I love it. And let me find out you gave my Apa some Ms. Campbell. Cause he sure is happy.*

Ms. Campbell: *lol don't worry bout that little girl*

Aaliyah: *well if you did thank youuuuuu lol*

After examining the inside of the car and driving it around the huge yard, Aaliyah went into the house to finally eat. She was beyond happy and wouldn't allow anything to steal her joy; not even her fake ass boyfriend.

***

Once Aaliyah had eaten and was now dressed she was ready to take her new ride for a spin. She convinced her Apa to let her go out for a while, but promising she would only pick up Venicia and be back soon. To her surprise he agreed and she couldn't wait. When she pulled up to Venicia's house, she was already outside waiting on her best friend to pull up. Venicia was dressed pretty simple but looking cute in a pair of ripped jeans and a shirt that spelled Barbie across the front. Aaliyah couldn't help but laugh because she was dressed in similar garments. She was also wearing ripped jeans, only she wore a spaghetti strapped Dolce & Gabbana top with a brown leather biker coat.

"Oooh bitch this shit bomb." Venicia chimed.

"No fuck the car. Bitch let me find out yo mama gave my Apa some?" Aaliyah smirked.

"She say she didn't but her ass sure was out late and came back beaming like she had hit the lottery." The girls laughed at Venicia's joke but dead ass.

Venicia hopped into the luxury vehicle and buckled her seat belt. Aaliyah pulled off slowly with the slightest clue as to where they were going.

“Let's go to BJ’s?” Venicia asked looking over at her friend.

“No fuck him. He basically left me for dead.

“But damn Liyah you atleast need answers. I mean what if something is wrong?”

“I doubt it. He got what he wanted Vee, and I'm not into chasing a nigga. I'm too fly for that shit.” Aaliyah joked doing a little dance in her seat.

“You aint never lied. That's why I gave up on Cali hoe ass. Fuck him. If he wanna continue to play games Ill play them with his ass. And besides I met a new boo.”

“Girl your a mess.”

For the remainder of the ride the girls gossiped and listened to the lastest music. When “Treat Me Like Somebody” Tink began to play threw her speakers, she pumped the music as loud as it went. Aaliyah loved her some Tink and this song was perfect for the way she was feeling. Her mind drifted off to BJ and she felt light weight hurt. She couldn't believe how he had played her. The thought of another woman having him pained her heart and that's exactly what she figured it was. She had made up this whole movie in her mind about some older woman being more experienced, coming in and doing things to BJ that she didn't know how do. She knew that getting over BJ wouldn't be easy but she would try her hardest to put him and his memories in the back of her mind.

CHAPTER 12 *(Brooklyn Jr.)*

"Trust no one..."

The week for BJ had been hard. He cried, slept and fed his body nothing but Conac. Manuel had tried to get him to eat something but each time he refused. In the last week he ate one pizza that lasted him four days. Because it was pretty much BJ, Pedro, Manuel, a cook and a maid that came by occasionally, there was no need to have a huge wake. Pedro had told BJ over and over that he wanted to be cremated and he wanted his ashes dumped into the ocean right where he had lost all of his friends. As bad as BJ wanted to bury his Papa, he understood his wishes so he did exactly as told. BJ and Manuel sailed out on BJ's yacht to the bahamas, and dumped the ashes in the Atlantic ocean as he wished. Every since the day, BJ locked himself back in his Papa's bedroom and slept his little life away. He had deactivated his social media account and powered his phone off. He didn't want to be bothered with the world.

Laying back on Papa's bed, BJ looked up from his bottle of Hennessy and noticed the envelope that his Papa had given him the night of his birthday. He never had a chance to open it, actually, he had forgotten all about it with all the things going on in his life. He lifted from the bed and retrieved the envelope. He walked out of the room and into Pedro's study so he could look over what he had finally seen as documents. He dumped the papers out onto the dresser. The short letter from his Papa is what stood out most.

Dear Papi,

I want you to look over this paperwork and understand what you have here is very important. Every piece of paper in this envelope is your life. This is where the road begins for you Mijo. I'm not saying you have to leave the house because you know you're welcome to stay forever, But you're a man now Papi so I want you to live a great life. You have many many assets and they have been waiting for you to turn eighteen. I know you're a smart man, but just incase you're puzzled about most of the stuff, I have someone that will help you. On the back of this letter is the number to my attorney. Take him all of the documents and he will explain it all. Hes also expecting your call. Inside the envelope is the deeds to a restaurant your father left you. There's two, one was left to your brother but since he died on the boat it's all yours. Also you have pink slips to 24 cars that were left from your mother father and grandmother. Theres three bank accounts with millions of dollars in each. Again one is from your mother, father, grandmother and a small account that I have been having for you since the accident. I need you to listen to me care fully... the deed to your grandmother's Mansion is also inside. There's twenty six bedrooms equipped with guards, maids and a chef. This is the home that we all occupied. In the four bedroom home thats built on the property, contains over a hundred fire arms for your protection. Now I must warn you, living in the home could possibly

alert the Cartel that you're still alive so it's up to you if you chose to occupy the home. Be very careful Mijo. I know you'll be ok, because I trained you well. I love you Papi and I know you'll make me proud. Remember one thing, TRUST NO ONE!

Your Papa,

BJ read the letter over and over again. He couldn't believe everything the envelope contained. Though him and his Papa lived well off, the fact of him being a 18 year old Billionaire, was unbelievable. It was all his. As much as he wanted to be happy, he didn't really care for the money, cars, and business, all he wanted was his Papa back. Over and over again BJ beat himself up. He often wondered if he had come home after the club would he have been able to save his Papa's life. Just the thought alone made him cry. BJ lifted from his seat and walked outside to the balcony. He looked out into the ocean and couldn't help but cry. He felt so alone. Over the course of the week, he had thought about Aaliyah nonstop. He knew she was probably upset with him but he couldn't even focus enough to reach out to her. The sounds of the waves crashing against shore was fucking with his mental, so he headed back inside. For the first time since the cremation, BJ had mustared up enough energy to go take a shower. Tonight he would chill in the beach house but first thing in the morning BJ would go speak with the lawyer. In the shower he thought long and hard. He finally made up his mind to move into the mansion. He wanted to leave the beach house because there were to many memories of his Papa that taunted him.

***

Walking into the 26 bedroom estate, BJ was ecstatic. He had seen many nice homes but nothing like the one he stood in at this very moment. The house was spick and span like someone had lived inside for all those years. All the furniture was covered in plastic, so that let BJ know that the home hadn't been occupied. From where he stood, he had a perfect view of the spiral staircase that swirled around at least three times. Out the big picture window he could see the huge statue that he'd always heard his Papa talk about. His Papa would always tell him that, the waterfall is where his Abuelita always sat. On the wall there was a enormous oil painting of his grandmother. He studied the picture for a long time. Ms. Lopez was beautiful. She reminded BJ of a slim version of Griselda Blanco. With the stories Pedro had told him, Ms. Lopez was indeed a split imagine of the *God Mother*. BJ had watched Cocaine Cowboys a million times, and each time he would picture his grandmother. After staring at the picture for some time, BJ headed upstairs. He was anxious to see the room that his mother occupied. Pedro had also told him about Cash and Nino having their own home but for some reason Cash kept her bedroom in her mother's home.

When he walked into the room, he was in awe at the bedroom set. Rubbing his hands across the Porcelain dresser, he made his way towards the closet. The closet alone looked like a one bedroom apartment. It was filled over capacity with clothing and shoes. Noticing the small square that was cut into the carpet BJ got curious. He lifted the rug and there sat a safe. It wasn't too big so he knew it only contained small items. With much force he lifted it out of the floor and sat it down. He took a seat on the floor and slid the safe in between his legs. He began fooling around with the combination lock. He entered his mother's birthday but it didn't work. He entered his dad birthday and again it didn't work. He sat quietly trying to contemplate what could it be, he thought long and hard. Finally trying his birthday, he heard the click. *Bingo!* He shook his head proud. When the safe opened up, he began fumbling with the items inside. There five stacks of money stacked neatly into rubber bands. There was also three firearms, and lots of jewelry. He pulled the jewelry out and examined it closely. There was ten rolex watches, two that he assumed belonged to his dad. There were several chains, from jesus pieces to crosses. Out of all the jewelry, three chains stuck out to him the most. A chain that read CASH, one that read Nino and a small cuban link that read BJ. looking over the chain that read BJ, BJ figured it had belonged to him. It was very small and of course because it had his initials. Feeling himself ready to break down, he quickly threw everything back into the safe and stood to his feet. He walked out of the closet and laid across his mother's bed. Not being able to hold it in, he began crying. And this was the reason he always wanted to be alone. He constantly cried and he wouldn't dare shed a tear infront of another soul. He didn't want people to think he was weak, showing emotions in front of them was out. The sound of the doorbell ringing knocked BJ out of his daze. *Who the fuck could that be?* He thought to himself. He went to his mother's safe and retrieved two firearms. Sticking them on each side of his waist, he made his way down the stairs. Looking threw the small glass windows, he noticed a man in all black. The earpiece he wore, made BJ think that it was a detective. Slowly opening the door, BJ stuck only half his body out.

"May I help you?"

"Yes Mr. Carter, I'm John. I'm the head of the security team that would be guarding your home from now on. I've been working with your grandmother for quite sometime." BJ only nodded his head. “There's four guards at the entrance at all times, six guards that patrol the estate and two sharp shooters on each side of the roof. From now on I recommend you keep guards with you at all times. All your vehicles are parked inside the garage except two. Here's the numbers to your cook and two maids. John said and handed BJ a sheet of paper. “One of the maids is new to work here because the one that was replaced passed away about three years ago. Also by every window in the home there’s a small button that would alert me when ever you need me. Also there's one in each bedroom and restroom. Now do you have any questions for me?” John asked BJ who looked as if he was trying to remember everything.

“No sir. If I do Ill ring you ok.”

“Okay Sir. Welcome home” John said and walked off. Just hearing the words made reality set in; this was now BJ’s home.

CHAPTER 13 *(Brooklyn Jr.)*

"My name is Papi, and if you fail to call me Papi, then yo' ass won't get an answer."

Several weeks later.....

BJ had been getting back into the swings of things. He had finally reached out to Cali who was happy to finally hear from his friend. BJ had caught Cali up on everything that had took place in his life over the last month and Cali was hurt for his friend. He also informed BJ that Aaliyah had been asking for him daily. BJ was so caught up in trying to settle into his home, he hadn't reached out to Aaliyah. He figured she had a new nigga by now so he let her go.

Tonight BJ was having a small kickback at the mansion but making sure to only invite friends from school and Young. He wasn't worried about his school mates because he had a security team that would blow a hole in anything that looked out of the ordinary. BJ had everything laid out for tonight. He had rented a shuttle that would pick everyone up and bring them up the hill. There was enough liquor to last a lifetime and a couple strippers would be coming through. At this very moment he was headed to a hair salon that Cali recommended because he needed his dreads retwisted badly.

When BJ walked into the hair salon, he had to admit, the shop was pretty nice. He stood still for a moment, taking in the decor. It had a teal and pink theme that actually looked cool together. He walked to the receptionist desk and checked in. Once he gave the young lady his name he took a seat in the waiting area. All the women in the entire salon were gawking at the young handsome man that stood before them. BJ only laughed at how thirsty the ladies were. Most of them appeared to be twice his age but that didn't seem to bother them one bit.

“BJ” a lady walked out and called his name. BJ studied her long and hard. She was breathtaking.

“Hi Im Monique, you could call me Mo.” She smiled. Shaking his hand, the beauty eyed him flirtatiously. “You could follow me this way.” She spoke and turned to head to her station. Walking away, BJ watched as her ass shifted from side to side. *Damn her ass fat.* He thought to himself in awe.

During the process of twisting BJs locks, Mo and BJ made small talk. She kept hinting around to see if he had a girl and that let him know she was feeling him. She also asked his age but apparently it didn't matter because she was still riding his swag. Once they were done, Mo spent BJ around in the chair to look at his locks in the over sized mirror. Mo had did wonders to BJ's hair. He was very impressed, shaking his head up and down in approval. He went into his pockets and pulled out his wad of cash. He handed her two hundred dollar bills.

“Keep the change ma.” He flirted.

“Thank you.” She smiled. “So I take it you like it?”

“Hell yeah, you hooked a nigga up. Good looking.”

“Anytime.”

As BJ got up to leave, Monique went for it. She asked him if she could hit him up sometimes and he agreed. Lickng her lips seductivily, she wanted to see what the young thug had in store for her. Pulling out his cell, they quickly exchanged numbers. BJ thought about inviting Mo to his kickback, but quickly thought against it. He wasn't one to baby sit a woman besides tonight he had a few honeys coming through.

BJ walked out the salon like he was that nigga and indeed he was. After he had gotten settled into his mansion, he had went to visit his restaurant his father had left him. He couldn't deny it, he was very impressed with the decor. Over the years, the establishment had been ran by Nino's right hand, Kellz who BJ hadn't met just yet. Pedro had let Kellz run the business instead of just shutting it down. Kellz agreed to keep it open and and taking care of the responsibility up until BJ turned 18.

***

"This muthafucka jumping!" Cali shouted to BJ over the music. Cali nodded his head to the sound of Future's "Stick Talk" as he reached over and grabbed a handful of LaTreva's ass. LaTreva was a typical round the way chick that flocked onto Cali in the club. She brought a few of her friends, and every last one of them wanted a piece of BJ. Even LaTreva was eye fucking BJ all night, and Cali noticed. Cali wasn't a hater by far, so he didn't sweat it.

"Hell yeah!" BJ shouted back to his boy right when three of the six strippers walked up on BJ. BJ was beyond the alcohol limit so he was extremely turnt up.

"I'll be right back." BJ looked over to Cali. With a simple head nod and a smirk, Cali laughed at his friend because he knew exactly what BJ was up to.

BJ led the three girls to his bedroom that Ms. Lopez had once occupied. When they walked in, BJ fell onto the bed but making sure not to spill the bottle of Ace he clutched tightly in his hand. One of the ladies bent down in front of him and began bouncing her ass. The other two ladies took a seat on each side of the bed and began groping BJ. BJ ran his free hand down one of the ladies thighs, right when the door flew open. Everyone in the room looked over towards the door and BJ had gotten the surprise of his life. Aaliyah stood there with so much hurt in her eyes. She shook her head left to right without a sound. "Liyah!" BJ called after her the moment she began to run out of the room. He lifted from the bed and chased her down the long hall. He caught her just in time before she went down the steps.

"Leave me the fuck alone BJ."

"Nah ma. You came here for a reason so holla at me."

"Now I wish I had never come." Aaliyah released the tears that were trying to break free. BJ looked at her and at the point he broke.

"Come here ma." He grabbed her hand and led her into one of the near by bedrooms. Aaliyah was hesitant but followed. When they approached the bedroom, BJ closed the door to give themselves some privacy.

"Look I apologize baby girl."

“Cut the bullshit Brooklyn. Is this why you just up and left me? So you could be single and free.”

“Nah ma it ain't like that.”

“Then tell me what it's like. Because it's been nearly two months and you haven't bothered to even reach out to me. Was my sex all you wanted?” Aaliyah cried harder at the thought of giving him her virginity.

“No ma. A nigga really love you.”

“How? How the fuck you love me but you just up and leave with out a simple phone call.” Aaliyah’s face softened as she looked at BJ for an explanation.

“Shit just got crazy in my life Liyah. Papa had died and I didn't know…..

“Oh my god.” Aaliyah covered her mouth with her hand. Her heart hit the floor at the mention of Pedro’s passing. “I'm so sorry Brooklyn. Oh my god I'm so sorry.”

“Its cool ma. It's not your fault.” BJ began to stress so he took a swig of the bottle to control his hurt. “When that shit happened ma, I distant myself from the world. I swear I didn't mean to hurt you.” BJ took another swig from the bottle. He was trying his hardest to keep the tears from falling. At this moment he was hurt because he was still shook over his Papa’s passing and he had hurt the one girl he knew he would forever love.

“So is this where you're living now?” Aaliyah asked and BJ only nodded.

“This house belonged to my….BJ was cut off at the the sound of the door opening. When he looked up it was Young. The two locked eyes but didn't speak one word. BJ felt weird about the way the guy looked at him. It was as if he was communicating something with his eyes.

"What does BJ stand for?" Young asked seriously.

"Why nigga. You don't know me."

"What the fuck does it stand for?!" Young shouted causing Aaliyah to jump. BJ stood to his feet because he didn't like how Young was demanding shit in front of his girl.

"Brooklyn Junior nigga." BJ said with his fist balled up. Young looked him over closely and shook his head right before walking out. *This nigga weird.* BJ thought to himself. Something was up with Young and BJ hoped he didn't have to body the nigga. *TRUST NO ONE Mijo.* Pedro's words played over and over in BJ's head. Because he knew how his parents lived, he also knew that they were loved by plenty and hated by many so he watched everything closely.

After the episode with Young, BJ shook off the thoughts and focused his attention back to Aaliyah. He knew that he had some making up to do and he would do what it took to get his girl back. Just seeing her pretty face today, showed BJ how much he missed her. He lifted from the bed and grabbed Liyah's hand. He walked down the stairs while pulling her close behind. When he made it to the party, he motioned with one hand for Aaliyah to give him one minute. He walked over to the socket and forcefully snatched out the plug that was connected to the DJ's equipment. Everyone stopped the moment the music stopped and focused in on BJ. Bj jumped on top of the marble counter with his bottle in his hand. Before speaking, he scanned the room looking over everyone in attendance. He took a swig from his bottle before speaking.

"From now on, nobody is to address me as BJ nor Brooklyn! My name is Papi and if you fail to call me Papi then yo ass won't get an answer. Party over!" BJ stood with his chest heaving up and down as everyone exited the house whispering. BJ could feel Aaliyah burning a hole in him but he refused to look her way. He would holler at her when he cleared his house out.

"Go to the room." He looked at Aaliyah. She shifted her weight to one side of her body and crossed her arms over her chest. "Do what the fuck I said!" BJ shouted. Smacking her lips Aaliyah stormed off.

"Aye Papi I'm bout to go fuck on LaTreva thick ass. Ill holla at you tomorrow."

"Aight fasho my nigga. I'm about to go up here and get my bitch back." Papi said and the guys laughed. "Do me a favor though. Holla at yo brother that nigga on some real weird shit Cali and I'm trying not to put a bullet between that nigga eyes."

"Ill holla at him foo. For now you just focus on yo girl." Cali said and they dapped each other up then departing ways.

CHAPTER 14 *(Aaliyah)*

"That's my baby and I'll do anything for him"

Laying in the bed with Papi, Aaliyah traced his tattoos gently with one finger. After a long night of having glorious sex, the two were on cloud nine. Aaliyah had missed Papi, and the feelings were mutual. Papi who laid on his back and stared at the ceiling, looked as if something was weighing heavy on his mind. Aaliyah wanted to ask him his thoughts, but she chose to let him share the details on his own.

Looking around the room that was now Papi's, Aaliyah, was very impressed with the decor. Just the bed alone had to cost a hundred thousand or near. Papi had told Aaliyah that it was the room his grandma had occupied when she was alive. He also gave Aaliyah a tour of the entire home, and explaining everything to her that his Papa had explained to him before he died. The sound of Aaliyah's ringing phone, made her stop in her tracks. She quickly jumped up and retrieved it from her handbag. Seeing that it was Venicia, she answered.

"Heyyyy Vee"

"Girl you need to get here asap. Your grandfather is on his way over."

"Oh my gosh. Okay." Aaliyah jumped from the bed and began dressing.

"What's the matter ma?" Papi asked worried.

"My Apa is on his way to Ms. Campbell's house. I have to go."

"How did you get here anyway?"

"Venicia brung me." Aaliyah said running around the room in a frantic. Papi jumped up and began dressing so he could quickly get her home.

***

Doing nearly 100 MPH on the highway, Aaliyah watched as Papi shifted the gears to his red F430 Spider. She had to hold the railing to keep from flying out the vehicle. Because she needed to get home, she didn't bother telling Papi to slow down. After the 25 minute drive that would have taken an hour, they were nearing Venicia's exit. "Shit!" Papi cursed, making Aaliyah turn in her seat to look behind them. Papi's first mind was to run, but he didn't want to put Aaliyah in harm's way. Papi pulled the vehicle over to the side of the road and waited for the police to approach his window.

"Can you roll the window down sir?" the officer asked politely. Papi did as told and waited for the next question.

"License and registration sir." Papi patted his pockets for his license. *Shit!* He cursed himself because he had forgotten his wallet on the dresser because he was in such a rush.

"My bad I forgot it at home. I know my number sir." Papi spoke looking over at the officer. A few moments later another patrol car pulled up.

"Can you give me your registration?" The officer asked. Papi reached over to retrieve it from the glove box. He handed the form to the officer and laid his head back on the seat.

"Sir I'm going to ask you to step out of the vehicle." The second officer asked walking up to the car. Papi looked over at Aaliyah and shook his head before stepping out. The officer walked

Papi over to the side, right when a female officer approached the spider and asked Aaliyah to step out as well.

"May I ask what's going on?" Papi asked.

"Well you don't have your licence, and the vehicle is coming back registered to a Cash Lopez. Our system is saying Cash Lopez is deceased.

"That's my mother sir."

"Well you should be fine." The officer stepped away from Papi and walked over to the car where there were four officers searching it.

After a few moments of searching the vehicle, the female officer yelled out. "We have a loaded firearm!" Again Papi shook his head then looked over at Aaliyah.

"So I guess this belongs to your dead mother." The officer spoke sarcastically waving the gun in Papi's face.

"Its mines!" Aaliyah shouted out causing Papi to nearly choke.

"Nah ma. Don't do that. I'm good." Papi spoke while eyeing Liyah.

"I don't want you to go to jail Brooklyn." Aaliyah cried out above a slight whisper.

"Don't do that ma. I'm good. I'll be out on bail." Papi fussed.

"Okay well since it belongs to both you guys, Ima gonna book you both." The officer said then forcefully snatched Papi to the patrol car. Aaliyah who silently cried, was more afraid of her grandfather than becoming arrested. *What the hell am I going to tell him.* She thought to herself as she was being escorted to a separate patrol car. Aaliyah watched Papi closely in the patrol car that was pulling off. He mouth the words "I love you" and that caused Aaliyah to break down.

***

Four hours later, Aaliyah had finally made a call to her grandfather. To her surprise he was calm, but Aaliyah knew better than to fall for it. She had been booked on a possession of a firearm and her Apa had promised he was on the way to post her bound. Mario possessed so much power, he was sure to get the case thrown out, however he wanted Aaliyah to suffer. Mario had everyone from CIA agents to judges in his pockets so a simple gun case wouldn't be a burden.

A couple more hours had passed by, and Aaliyah's name was called for release. She hesitantly walked out of the holding cell with a tear stained face. The entire time she spent in the cell, she was more worried about Papi. Making it to the front, she was given her property bag and told to walk down the hall where her grandfather awaited her. When she made it to the lobby, Mario was seated. He looked at her with such a venomous glare it caused Liyah to drop her head shamefully. Mario stood to his feet without a word and walked out of the station angry.

Once they hopped into the limo, Mario began to grill her.

"You will not leave the house for a long time child." Mario shook his head.

"I'm sorry Apa." Aaliyah began crying.

"Why the fuck are you riding around with guns Mija?"

"To protect myself." She looked into Mario's eyes, hopping he brought her story.

"Since when do you have to protect yourself?"

"I'm not stupid. I know what you do for a living. You think I don't know why you always send guards with me?" She asked seriously. Mario was stunned by her words but he didn't utter a word.

"Since you've bought my car, and the detail hasn't been with me as much, I bought the gun Apa. I'm sorry, I just wanted to be safe."

"Yes I understand. But you should have come to me Liyah. I would have gotten you a registered gun. Now you have a fucking case. What if you go to jail? Huh? Do you know what those women would do to you in jail?" Mario taunted her. Aaliyah remained quiet and looked out of the window in such a deep thought. Her mind drifted to Brooklyn. She prayed he would be okay. She didn't want him to get in any trouble and if she had to do it again, she would.

Pulling up to her home, Aaliyah went to her bedroom to call Cali. she wanted to ask him had Papi called and even see if he needed to make bail. With Mario's strict orders about not leaving the house, Aaliyah would just leave willingly. She knew her grandfather would punish her, but she didn't care because she wanted to go place a bond for Papi.

"Liyah what's up ma?"

"Hey Cali. Ummm...has Papi called you?" She asked. Cali chuckled lightly because even Aaliyah had called BJ by his new name.

"Yeah I'm with Manuel right now. Were on our way to pick Papi up now ma."

"Yes thank god." She closed her eyes and her mind was now at ease.

"He told me what you did too you a rida for real." Cali laughed and made Aaliyah smile.

"That's my baby and I'll do anything for him."

"Thats whats up ma. Cali smiled as if Aaliyah could see him through the phone. Just the thought of her being a ride or die chick made him wish he had got the chance. Aaliyah had always seemed square and quiet, however he knew she was off limits. "That nigga need somebody like you to keep him copastestic Liyah, so don't eva give up on him. We pulling up now, Ima have him call you as soon as they release him.

"Okay." They disconnected the line. Aaliyah headed to the restroom to began her shower. She needed to scrub last night's sex off her and she was beyond tired.

CHAPTER 15 *(Brooklyn Jr. aka Papi)*

"This shit is a bit too much"

The next morning…

Papi woke up bright and early so he could get dressed and ready for his day. A guy named Allen who was being detained in the station's cell with Papi, had giving him the number to an attorney that was proclaimed the best in town. Papi was gonna do everything in his power to get the case dismissed for Aaliyah. Even if he had to do the time, he didn't sweat it; as long as Liyah was straight.

After finishing his shower, Papi got dressed and headed for the front door. The moment he pulled the door open, Young was standing there with a look of worry. Papi rubbed his hands threw his locks and sighed in annoyance.

"Man what's the deal with you? And how the fuck you get in my gate brah?" Papi asked while holding the door open. He made a mental note to holla at his staff.

"I need to holla at you Papi." Young pushed passed him and went to take a seat in the foyer. Papi closed the door and followed behind him.

"Look I apologize at how I came at you the other night, but all this shit is crazy to me. I used to work for Ms. Cash and Ms. Lopez." Young looked at Papi and waited for his reaction. Seeing the astonished look on his face, he continued. "Man they took me in with open arms at 19 years old. I was suppose to be on that Yacht, but because I was out collecting money, I was scheduled to hop on the second ship." Young dropped his head. Papi looked over at him and his heart went out to him. He knew there was truth behind his story because Pedro had told him about the second Yacht that was suppose to aboard the rest of the crew. And now that he mentioned it, he also remembered Pedro mentioning Young's name a few times. "All these years I thought you were dead B..Papi." Young quickly corrected himself. "Where have you been living?" He asked with so much hurt in his voice.

"I was living on the beach with Pedro."

"Pedro?" Young asked excited at the mention of Pedro's name. Young had missed his crew dearly and if he had to just have Pedro and Papi in his life then that would make him feel closer to his friends that were now gone. "Where is he papi?" Young asked walking towards the door.

"He's dead." Papi quickly dropped his head. Young froze in his steps then turned to look at Papi.

"What happened?"

"He passed in his sleep. When I got home he was dead." Papi said just above a whisper. "He left me an envelope with the deed to this house and all my parents cars and shit. He died about two months ago at our beach house."

"Damn man I'm sorry to hear that." Young's heart went out to Papi. Young knew that Pedro was all Papi had because the entire crew was dead. He wished that he could have found the two many years ago and maybe it would have eased his heart. Young was devastated without his friends. "If you need anything Papi don't ever hesitate to hit me. I don't give a fuck what it is. Ill kill any muthafucka that ever cross you starting with their grandmother. Your family was my family nephew and I swear I'll die for you." Young said and walked towards the front door. Before he walked out, he gave Papi one last look. “Don't ever hesitate to bang my line man.” Young said and Papi nodded. Once Young was out of sight, Papi headed for his car, hopped in and googled the address to the attorneys office. Just knowing Young was now in his life, it made him feel close to his parents.

***

“Sir do you have an appointment?” The receptionist asked Papi as he walked to the front desk.

“No but I got money ain't that’s enough?”

“I'm sorry sir but she's extremely busy.”

“What the fuck you mean, it….” Papi was cut off by a caramel skinned beauty. She looked much older than Papi but that didn't stop him from looking. Her skin was wrinkle free, her smile lit up the entire room and her long silky hair made her look like an Indian goddess.

“It's ok Michelle, I'll see him.” The lady told the receptionist. She turned to walk towards her office and with one finger she motioned for Papi to follow.

Once they walked into the office the attorney took her seat behind her desk. Papi took a seat and looked at her with lust in his eyes. It was something about the way the attorney looked at him that made him feel weird. She wasn't looking at him as if she wanted to blow his rocks off, It was more like she was studying him.

“Look, me and my girl got pulled over and they found a gun. One gun two bodies, I don't even know if that's possible mamm.” Papi jumped right into it. He was trying to hurry up with the meeting because she was making him feel uneasy. “Do you hear me?” Papi asked annoyed.

“humm..oh..Im so sorry.” she hadn't heard a word Papi said. “I'm sorry but it's something about you that's very familiar.”

“Nah you don't know me ma.” Papi smirked and stood to leave.

“Wait! I'm sorry, I'll help you. What's your name?” The attorney asked. *Trust No one Mijo* Pedro’s words played in Papi’s head. Papi wanted badly to lie about his name, but because he needed her help he chose to be honest. “Its Papi.”

“Well Papi, I dont think thats the name on the case.”

“My bad ma. Its Brooklyn Carter Jr.” The moment he spoke the words, the attorney began choking on her spit. She eyed Papi curiously and tears began to weld up in her eyes. Without being able to hold them back, the tears came pouring down her angelic face.

“BJ!” She shouted with tears streaming down her face. She ran over to him and wrapped her arms around him tightly. Papi who was still curious, remained silent until she explained to him what was going on. He broke the hug and stepped back. He needed answers and he needed them now.

“Who are you ma?”

“Bree...Bree…” She couldn't speak because she was too busy sobbing. Papi gave her a moment to gather herself then took a seat.

“Im Breelah, Breelah Carter.” Papi’s eyes shot open wide at the mention of his aunt’s name. He began shaking his head as he mumbled the words “this shit is a bit too much”

Many times, Pedro had mentioned Breelah but he had never seen any pictures of her in Papa’s home. He told Papi how Breelah was the first person to throw him in the air and the first person to ever make him laugh. Breelah Carter was the only sister and the baby of the three, Brooklyn, Bronx and Breelah. Bronx, had went missing right before the wedding. Pedro had done everything in his power to find Bronx, but each time, he came up short.

"So where have you been BJ?" Breelah asked pulling Papi from his thoughts. He looked up at her and prepared himself to tell her the story of how he had survived and up until now.

***

After Papi left his aunt's office, he headed to the restaurant to finally have a sit down with Kellz. He promised Breelah he would stay in contact with her. Breelah had also informed him she would get Aaliyah off Scot free and free of charge. Papi felt great knowing he had someone on this earth that he knew would love him like his Papa had. It was like fate that the man in the cell had given him the number to the office.

Looking in his rearview, Papi had nearly forgotten that the detail was following him. He hated the fact that John had always ordered him to be followed. To John it was only for his safety because he had seen the Lopez Cartel go through so much. To Papi it was like he was being baby sat and the shit annoyed his soul.

Pulling up to the establishment, Papi was applauded. From the outside the restaurant looked extravagant, he could only imagine what the inside looked like. He pulled his car up to the valet and hopped out a proud owner. He made his way into the restaurant in search of Kellz. Kellz was his father's right hand man and bestfriend. Kellz too, was scheduled to aboard the second yacht for the ceremony but he too didn't make it. When Papi walked in, he was blown back at the scenery. The restaurant was more beautiful than he had imagined. He watched on as the patrons sat on pillows and ate their meals. He also noticed everyone that was seated without food, had laptops in their hands, which was how you ordered your meal. The smell of fruit lingered through the air, as people smoked on hookah. All the workers wore silk based chinese dresses and the men wore two piece chinese print suits. *This shit fly.* He smiled to himself at his father's accomplishment. The restaurant was called *Mahealani*, which was named after Brooklyn's Sr. beloved mother. Pedro hasn't gave Papi much info about his other grandparents, however he did mention that they were heavy in the drug business before dying at the hands of a ruthless king pin named Big AL.

"Hi may I help you?" A caucasian woman approached Papi with a huge smile.

"Yes I'm looking for Kellz." Papi kept it brief.

"Okay and your name sir?"

"Brooklyn Carter Jr." Papi said giving her his government name. He knew that the name would cause a reaction and it was indeed the reason he had given it to her. Just like he thought she stood puzzled.

"Um..Um..okay. I'll be right back." She rushed off towards the back. Papi didn't wait, he simply followed behind the woman. Reaching the fifth door down the long hall, Papi walked in and for the first time he came face to face with Kellz. The two stared at each other long and hard and not saying a word. Looking at Papi was like looking at his dear bestfriend. Kellz shook his head but not once taking his eyes off Papi. Pedro and Kellz had stayed in contact but Pedro didn't want Kellz around because he didn't want to bring any harm to Papi. He knew that the Cartel knew Kellz was still alive and he didn't want the heat coming Papi's way. He agreed to let Kellz run the restaurant up until Papi turned 18 then the establishment would be his. Kellz agreed and had been doing a great job.

"Got damn you look just like Nino." Kellz said calling Brooklyn Sr. by his street name.

"I've been getting that a lot lately." Papi laughed. Kellz walked over and gave him a manly hug then told him take a seat.

"I couldn't wait to see you BJ."

"With all do respect Kellz, I'd appreciate if you call me Papi."

"Hahaha if you ain't Cash's fucking son." Kellz laughed making Papi smile. He had heard about his mother's cocky but smooth demeanor. Over and over Pedro had also told him, he looked like his father but had his mother's attitude. "Papi it is young nigga." Kellz laughed again but shaking his head. Just looking at Papi he knew shit was about to get real, just as it did when his parents were alive.

CHAPTER 16 *(Aaliyah)*

"Dat e Nght"

Aaliyah had finally been able to leave the house. After three weeks of punishment, her Apa had finally let up. Of course with Ms. Campbell in the picture she knew it wouldn't be hard. Lately, Mario and Ms. Campbell had been getting mighty cozy. Every since Mario had divorced, he had been wilding out with plenty women. It was something about Ms. Campbell that Mario had a weak spot for and like always Aaliyah used it to her advantage. Tonight Papi was taking Aaliyah to club Exclusive because he wanted to speak with the owner. Though it was business, to Aaliyah it was a much needed date. It was the first night Aaliyah and Papi would be seeing each other since the arrest. Everyday the two had talked on the phone and on instagram.

Finishing the last touches on her makeup Aaliyah fished for her ringing phone. She knew that it was Papi by the ringtone so she quickly answered.

"Hey baby." She cooed into the phone.

"Im outside Stinka."

"Okay here I come." She said anxiously. She walked back into Venicia's room and grabbed her purse. Venicia was sound asleep just that fast, something that she had been doing a lot lately. She made sure not to disturb her sleep, because she looked so peaceful.

When Aaliyah walked out the house, she smiled at the beautiful ride that was parked out front. Papi stepped out of the car and opened Aaliyah's door and waited for his princess to climb in. Once he was inside, he looked over her admiring her nightwear. She was rocking a sexy white bodycon dress that was made by Herve Leger. The dress hugged her body to a perfection. Her hair was pulled back into a nice sleek ponytail making her jaw structure stand out. She smiled shyly exposing her one dimple and little did she know, she was driving him crazy.

“You looking sexy as a muthafuck Stinka.” Papi said grabbing the bulge in his pants. Aaliyah had his dick rock hard, and if it wasn't for the meeting being so important he would have skipped out and headed home to make love.

“Thank youuuu baby. You looking good too.” Aaliyah also admired his look. His locks hung down falling over his shoulders and he was rocking a Armani blazer with a pair of stone washed jeans. The outfit looked hip but classy and Aaliyah was proud that she could call him her man. Papi reached over and kissed her with so much passion. He had missed his baby just as much as she missed him. The facetime calls were cool, but they needed each other in the flesh. Breaking the kiss, Papi reached over and retrieved the red velvet box that he had been dying to give her. Her eyes lit up at the sight of the box. She knew it wasn't a ring because it was too big, however she knew it was jewelry. Papi handed Liyah the box and sat back. When she opened it, she smiled widely letting him know she loved it. It was a gold necklace with a nameplate that read Papi covered in diamonds. Because the necklace was short, it went perfect with her dress.

“Its beautiful! Thank you Papi.” She said and the two began laughing.

“I'm not done ma.” He said and went into his pocket and pulled out a small box. Aaliyah couldn't hide the smile if she tried. Opening the box, Papi looked Aaliyah in the eyes. He licked his full sexy lips before speaking and that made Aaliyah melt in her seat. When he opened the box, it was like a disco ball was above them because the diamonds lit up the entire ride. They were breathtaking.

"Now this ain't no engagement or nothing ma, so don't get to going crazy." Papi chuckled. "Just know that the day I make you my wife, your ring gone be twice this size and so icy girl you gone make anybody that walk by sneeze." They both laughed. "Since the day I saw you in the hall at school, Liyah, I had to have yo ass. I know I gave you a hard time in the beginning and I'm sorry ma. This ring is a promise that I'll be here forever. I don't give a fuck what we go through, you'll always be my stinka baby." Papi handed Aaliyah the ring. "Read it." He said and she did just that. Inside the ring it was engraved *"My Ridah"* Aaliyah lips moved as she read but not a single word came out. She was still high and on cloud nine off of everything he had said. "That day we got arrested, I aint gone lie I was mad as hell at you for trying to take that gun case but I have to admit ma, that was some gangsta ass shit. That let me know right there how much you love a nigga and you not only my right hand but you my Ridah as well. I love you Liyah." Papi said and slid the ring onto her finger. Aaliyah was speechless. She didn't have to say a word because the tears that ran down her face spoke volumes.

After getting the ring on, Papi wiped her tears away, then cupped her face in his hands. He placed a genuine kiss on her forehead and told her tonight was their night. Looking out of the window, Liyah noticed they were pulling up to the club. She quickly gathered herself and smiled joyful at Papi. When the Rolls Royce came to a halt, the driver stepped out and opened the door for her. Not even one minute out the vehicle, and already Liyah was turning heads. Everyone looked on at the couple as if they were some sort of celebrities, when in fact they were two young and innocent teens; well at least for now.

Stepping into the dimly lit club, Aaliyah took in the atmosphere and sighed a breath of relief. Tonight she was feeling good and looking fabulous and she wanted to put everything in the back of her mind. She wanted to enjoy her night with her prince then go to his mansion for a night of intimate sex. To Liyah, it was just a regular date, but little did she know Papi would be making the biggest move of his career.

***

When Aaliyah and Papi walked into the VIP, everything was laid out for them. There was a bucket of ice, two glasses, two bottles of Ace and a bottle of D'usse cognac. Cali was already in attendance with Young and Liyah smirked at the two nestled up in the corner with chicks all in their grills. Liyah hated how Cali did her friend but because it wasn't her business, she ignored him and took her seat. Papi walked over to them and gave them a pound but making sure not to go far. He wanted to keep a watchful eye on his baby. Aaliyah grabbed her glass and began to pour herself a drink. She bopped her head to Young MA's "Ooouuu" looking around the crowded club. Aaliyah loved this club. Though she only been there once, she loved the atmosphere. Whoever the owner was, she knew they put a pretty penny into the establishment. The VIP section was sectioned off with Red mirrored glass. The booths were made of Canopies, and the floor was bullet proof glass that showed the entire first floor. Everyone seemed to be in tune with the music and the way the security prowled around, she knew the chances of drama were slim to none.

"Nephew!!! A male voice called out making Liyah turn in her seat. The man walked over to Papi and gave him a manly hug. Though Liyah had never seen him before, he and Papi looked happy to see each other. He appeared to be in his late forties but he was very handsome. He was well dressed and the jewelry he wore, told Liyah he was a dope boy most definitely. When Papi noticed Liyah looking, he snagged at the gentleman's arm and pulled him over.

"Unc this my wifey Aaliyah, Liyah this my uncle Kellz." Papi introduced the two. Kellz reached out and hugged her and she smiled shyly.

"Damn nephew, were her ma dukes, a aunty something?" Kellz asked laughing.

"Nah unc yo wife aint bout to kill me." Papi said and they all laughed.

Every since the meeting at the restaurant, Papi had been in touch with Kellz. He also agreed to let Kellz continue to run his restaurants, in Miami and in California as long as Kellz paid him his dough. Because Kellz had been his pops best friend, and he had been holding down the restaurant's, Papi gave him 30% of the earnings.

"There that nigga go right there nephew." Kellz said nodding his head. Papi looked in the direction towards the older man. He had on a very expensive suit and his huge belly looked as if his pants would burst open any moment. When he noticed Kellz and Papi he walked over to them with a wide grin. He shook Kellz hand then focused in on Papi. He studied him long and hard before speaking.

"And you must be Papi?" He said but watching him closely. Aaliyah stood on the sideline quietly but she payed close attention to every detail.

"Yeah thats me." Papi smirked cockly. It was something about the way he said it, that made Aaliyah look in his direction. "Now are you gonna give me what I want?" Papi asked looking the man dead in his eyes. He shook his head and looked at Papi as if he had lost his mind. He concentrated really hard before speaking.

"Now youngsta. This here place aint cheap. Do you see this place? Do you see this crowd?" The man said. Aaliyah was puzzled as to what was going on. But knowing her place, she still remained quiet.

"Man just name your stake old man." Papi said taunting the guy.

"A quarter of a million." the man challenged.

"I'll give you a whole million, now get the fuck up out my face and go start my paper work." Papi said and mugged the man. The man stood there stunned, not knowing what to say next. He couldn't understand how could such a young man his age make such a great offer. Old man Bill didn't expect Papi to bite for the quarter of a mill, and here it was the young thug had proved him wrong.

Old man Bill, walked off towards his office. Papi grabbed the small of Aaliyahs back and told her he'll be right back. He didn't even give her a chance to respond, he quickly excused himself from Liyah and Kellz who stood to the side still laughing. Aaliyah walked over and took a seat on the plush sofa. She poured herself a drink as she contemplated what was going on. She knew Papi was rolling in dough but she never thought he had enough money to blow a million dollars as if it was nothing. The look in Papi's eyes, told Liyah that whatever it was he wanted, and he wanted it bad. She wished he would tell her what was going on, but he was in a whole other mind frame. She'd patiently waited until he was ready to bring her up to speed.

CHAPTER 17 *(Brooklyn Jr. aka Papi)*

"Bitch, I'm the man. Hoe, I'm the man"

Papi walked around club exclusive the new owner. This was the best investment he could have ever made in his lifetime. Most people would think he did it for the money, but he did it because the club held much sentimental value. Kellz had explained to Papi that the club was once his mother's and it had been auctioned off. He also told him many stories of how his mother ran the establishment. It was once called club "Juice" when it belonged to his mother. However that would also change. Papi had plans on naming the club "Empire" because it was built from his family's empire. Papi wanted the club so bad, and Bill wouldn't began to understand. *Stupid muthafucka.* Papi thought to himself because he would have paid three times the price if he had to.

Too much on my mind right now
I'm on the grind right now
Looking for me, sucker, then I need to be found right now
I got my nine right now
Bitch, I'll blow your mind right now
I ain't fucking around right now
Better get in line right now
Or fuck around and die right now
Hope you understand that

Bitch, I'm the man, hoe, I'm the man you know I'm the man......

Walking out of Bill's office Papi sang to the lyrics of 50 Cent "I'm The Man". Right now he felt like that nigga and he was untouchable. He was young and rich and niggas couldn't walk in his shoes if they wore his size. He made his way threw the crowd towards the restroom because of all the alcohol his body had consumed, he had to take a leak bad as a mutha. The establishment was big with a number of restrooms throughout the entire club, so when Papi walked up to the nearest one it was unoccupied. He ran in quickly because at any moment he felt he would pee his pants. He quickly unfastened his jeans and let his huge dick pour the alcoholic liquid from his body. *Weww* he sighed in relief. Once he was done, he shook himself and began to zip his pants. Out of nowhere he felt a pair of hand grab as his jeans, he quickly turned around thinking he was caught with his pants down literally. "Hey sexy" The familiar voice spoke so seductively he couldn't help but smirk. Turning to look at the beauty, he was stunned at her boldness. Before the blink of an eye, she pulled his piece out from his jeans and dropped to her knees. Taking his massive dick into her mouth Papi moaned out in pure ecstasy. *Aaliyah!* He thought to himself and tried to pull back. Monique knew what he was doing so she quickly deep throated him and began forcefully sucking as if her life depended on this blow job. *"Fuckkk!* He growled because she was taking him to a place he had never been before. He grabbed her head and pumped into her mouth with aggression. She sucked, slurped and nearly swallowed him whole. "Shit ma Im bout to cu... fuck Im bout to cummm.." He howled. Seconds later he released in her mouth and she swallowed every ounce of his thick cum. She then stood to her feet and fixed her dress. As bad as Papi wanted to bend her over, he had to get back to Liyah before she came looking for him. Mo smiled widely and told him. "Don't be a stranger" then walked out as quietly as she had come. Papi leaned his head back on the cold wall and tried his best to regain himself. Once he was composed, he walked out the restroom as if nothing ever happened.

***

Walking out of the restroom, it was like Monique had vanished. Papi made his way back to the VIP so he could get his girl and leave. He had gotten what he came for so he was ready to go home and celebrate. Walking up the stairs, he had a clear view of Liyah in the VIP section. There was a guy in her face and whatever he was saying had Aaliyah smiling as if she was enjoying it. From her body language he could tell she was a bit tipsy but that wasn't an excuse. He was furious. Without a word, Papi walked over to the two and punched the guy so hard he stumbled back falling into a pile of women that were in a circle dancing.

“Brooklyn!” Aaliyah cried out but it fell onto deaf ears. Papi walked over to the guy and whipped his pistol out. He stuck the gun into the guy's mouth forcefully as his face scrunched up with anger.

“Nigga, if I ever see you in my fucking club Ima blow yo fucking wig back.” Papi said with the barrel of the gun in the guy's mouth not giving him a chance to respond. Kellz and Cali ran over to the altercation with their guns drawn, ready for the war. However, the guy was defeated. He shook so bad, Papi thought any minute he would shit his pants.

“Brooklyn please!.” Aaliyah screamed out knocking Papi from his thoughts.

"Man take yo ass to the car Liyah!." He barked at her slightly shaking her up. In the process of him focusing his attention on Liyah, the guy got up and left the VIP without another word.

"You good my nigga?" Cali asked concerned. Papi didn't reply he simply shook his head in annoyance. Kellz stood back quietly making sure nobody got buck. "Let's roll." Papi said to Kellz and Cali and the three of them left the club.

Once outside, Papi dapped Kellz and Cali up and told them he'll holla at them tomorrow. He was still furious at the situation with Liyah but he tried his hardest not to let it show. When he hopped into the back seat of the car, Liyah looked up at him with pleading eyes. Papi turned his head and laid back in his seat; he didn't have shit to say. He had the whole night planned out for him and his girl but the way he was feeling, he just wanted to be left alone. His initial plans were to go on a night sail, on his Yacht that his Papa had bought him for his birthday but that quickly changed. Though the driver was making his way to the ocean, Papi decided he would just occupy the bedroom on the ship and call it a night.

Forty five minutes later, Papi and Liyah pulled up to the yacht. Papi exit the vehicle stubbornly still not saying one word. Looking at her pouty face, made him want to submit but he wouldn't dare give in. Aaliyah was all the way wrong and very disrespectful in his eyes. For one, she shouldn't have had a nigga in her face, as a matter of fact why the fuck was he even in Papi's section to begin with. *Fuck her!* He thought heading into the master bathroom to scrub Monique's juices off his dick. He had to admit, that Mo's head game was official and soon he would try it again.

***

In the middle of the night, Papi woke up out his sleep. Throughout the night he stirred in his slumber because his princess wasn't by his side. All though he was mad at her, he missed her little ass even in his dreams. He lifted out of bed and headed in the other room where he expected her to be asleep. When he reached the door she wasn't in bed so he made his way around the ship to find her. After searching every crack and crevice, Liyah wasn't nowhere in site. Papi walked outside to the deck to get some air, because now he was stressing harder than before. Before he was completely out the door, he stopped in his tracks. He crossed his arms over each other and watched the beauty before him. The nights air was breezy and the lighting from the moon beamed down giving the ocean a certain glare that would put one in a trance. Aaliyah was leaning over the railing and looking out into the night. The slight breeze blew her hair making her look like a guardian angel. Papi began to listen to the lyrics of a song that was playing soft threw the yachts bluetooth. For some apparent reason, he could tell the song was for him.

Been waiting on that sunshine
Boy, I think I need that back
Can't do it like that
No one else gon' get it like that
So why argue? You yell, but you take me back
Who cares when it feels like crack?
Boy you know that you always do it right
Man, fuck your pride, just take it on back, boy
Take it on back boy, take it back all night

Just take it on back, take it on back
Mmm, do what you gotta do, keep me up all night
Hurting vibe, man, and it hurts inside when I look you in your eye

Kiss it, kiss it better, baby
Kiss it, kiss it better, baby

Not being able to hold out any longer, Papi walked up to Liyah and grabbed her around her waist. He slowly spent her around then lifted her body to place her on top of the railings. She looked him in the eyes with so much pain and desire at the same time. Papi looked into her eyes, and it was like he could see her soul. Her heart yearned for him. He gently kissed her then in one quick motion he slipped her silk gown over her head. It was now time to give himself to her and free his mind. All night, he had been thinking of his club. But something was much more on his mind that he hadn't told anyone in all these years, not even his Papa; he wanted to find out who murdered his parents and when he did, he was gonna murder everyone in his way.

CHAPTER 18 *(Brooklyn Jr. aka Papi)*

"This shit is crazy"

Two weeks later….

Papi woke up to the sound of the intercom above his bed. He was very annoyed because he had finally closed his eyes not even two hours ago. Last Night he was out at his club doing work on the building. He had finally put up his sign that read *'Empire'* and he also did a few touches on the inside. Three weeks from today he was throwing the biggest bash of the century, his grand opening and it was gonna be lit.

"Sup John?" He answered groggy into the speaker.

"Good morning Mr. Carter. Young is here to see you should I let him threw?"

"Aight let him threw." Papi said then lifted out the bed. He went into the restroom to brush his teeth then headed down stairs to unlock his front door. Because John and the other guards had been knowing Young personally, they would always let him come thru the gates but because it was to early they knew Papi would throw a fit.

When Papi opened the door, Young was already on the porch waiting. He dapped him up and let himself in the home. He then walked out the side door to the yard, and that let Papi know he wanted to discuss serious business. Papi followed Young out of the door and prepared himself for the conversation he was unsure of. When he got outside, Young was seated on the bench in front of the waterfall. The look on his face told Papi he missed his friends dearly. Every time he sat here, he would reminisce on his dear friend, Ms. Lopez, because he knew this is where her and Pedro sat daily.

"Whats up Young? Whats on yo mind big bro?" Papi said taking a seat besides him.

"I need a huge favor man?" Young said with pleading eyes.

"And what's that?" Papi asked with his eyebrows raised.

"Look I know you might not want to do this but hear me out. Before you say no, just give it some thought. This is a major move but it would pay off good?"

"Holla at me man."

"I need you to holla at Gustavo ." Young said praying he wouldn't say no.

"Who the fuck is Gustavo Young?"

"The Plug."

"Nigga my granny was the plug and she dead." Papi lightly chuckled. But Young on the other hand was serious as a heart attack.

"True, Ms. Lopez was the plug, matter of fact she was the entire plug of the whole fucking Miami but remember she had to get her work from somewhere."
"But why you want me to holla at him?"

"Because he won't fuck with us. I ain't had no work in a week and that shit killing me. Plus this nigga Que only sends me twenty at a time. But this nigga hadn't answered his phone in months" Just the mention of Que's name, had Papi's antennas up. His Papa had told him all about Que and the parts he played in the Lopez Cartel. Que worked for Ms. Lopez for many years. When she got knocked by the feds, he began to work for Cash as she took on Ms. Lopez's empire. Pedro had also told him about the love affair that his mother and Que once had, not to mention the the love triangle he had had with Breelah as well. Every single time his Papa spoke on the Empire, Papi would get a kick out of the wild and amazing stories. Cash had broken things off with Que the moment she fell in love with Nino. Breelah and Que had later hooked up and fell madly in love. On numerous occasions, Papi had asked Pedro if he had contact to Que so he could reach out to him, but it was like Que had fell off the face of the earth. He was happy to have found Kellz and Young but he wouldn't mind finding Que because he held a special part in the Lopez family. Since Pedro's passing, Papi had been feeling empty and lonely. Now that Breelah was around, he felt a little more love and comfort. As a matter of fact, Papi had made up his mind to holla at Bree about moving in. He wanted his aunt near by and why not? He had 25 other bedrooms that weren't occupied.

"If he knew you were Ms. Lopez grandson, he would for sure sale to you and at least 100 at a time if not more. Young said breaking Papi's train of thoughts. "Yo Gee Moms used to get two to three hunnit at a time. That nigga and Ms. Lopez was close as a mutafucka. I mean come on man, this shit is in yo blood line. I know yo little ass rich now, but you'll be eating five times better." Papi watched Young as he spoke but his mind was elsewhere. He hadn't thought much about getting in the game so he didn't want to jump in head first. The thought of him making five times the money sounded tempting but he had to give it more thought.

"And where this nigga at?" Papi asked out of curiosity.

"Columbia." Young said it as if Columbia was across the street.

"I don't know man. I never thought about getting into that game Young."

"I'll teach you lil bro. I mean shit you got a whole army already behind you. And knowing who your parents were, a muthafucka wouldn't dare test you." Young spoke surely "just give it some thought." Young said and stood to his feet to leave. He dapped Papi and made his way to his car, leaving Papi in his thoughts. For many years Papi had promised his Papa he wouldn't dare enter the drug game but his Papa wasn't here. He closed his eyes and said a silent prayer asking God and his Papa to forgive his thoughts. He made his way into the house to get some much needed rest because as of now, his mind was running a mile a minute.

***

"How you doin ma?" Papi asked Monique walking into her home. Thinking about her head game, he reached out to her for more. Aaliyah was at school and he hadn't seen her in almost a week and he was in need of some loving. Papi loved Aaliyah to death but at times it was as if he was dating a little girl. Her grandfather was too damn strict for his likings. Papi was now in the big leagues, getting major money so he needed a grown ass woman to occupy his time.

"Whats up with you Zaddy? I see you finally called." Mo smirked.

"Shit after that shit you served a nigga with at the club, you been on my mind."

"Is that right? So I'm guessing yo little girl friend can't do it like me." Mo said seductively walking off towards her bedroom. She stopped at the entrance of the hall and with one finger she motioned for him to follow. Monique knew what she was doing.

She put an extra switch in her hips and her 30 inch weave swayed side to side. She was a sexy stallion and every man's fantasy.

Monique, wasted no time undressing Papi. She knew what he had come for so there was no sense in wasting time. For the first time since they had met, she wanted a piece of his beefcake. After she gave him a full demonstration head job in the bathroom of Empire, she had been yearning for his touch. Mo was head over heels over the young boss. She often wondered if she could snag him and make him her man. Even though Aaliyah was a pretty girl, Mo knew she was inexperienced so she wasn't a threat. Nearly reaching her mid forties, Mo, was tired of being alone. The last rich nigga she thought she had was with Brooklyn Sr. aka Nino, that's until Cash Lopez stole him right from under her nose. Every since, she had been playing men left and right and vowed from that day, it was fuck niggas. Monique was your typical round the way chick, who had slept with nearly every man in Miami. She had been intimate with Que, Nino and even a few of Cash's male friends. She was one of Cash's Barber in her all female Barber shop called "Trap Gyrl". A little while before the explosion, Cash had literally went upside of Mo's head for some snake shit she had done, once again. Mo left the shop and ended up opening her own. Now that Cash was dead, she was that bitch in Miami and she loved having the title.

Standing asshole naked massaging his manhood, Papi wide eyed Mo with lust in his eyes. He wanted to get knee deep in her pussy and bounce because he had to meet Young to cook up his work. Just as Young said, The columbians sold Papi the birds on the strength of Ms. Lopez. It had been a couple weeks and Papi was already the man in town known for having the best work in town.

Mo layed back on the bed, and began fingering herself. With her tongue touching her top lip, she seductively rubbed her warmth preparing for what she had been longing for from Papi from the moment he sat in her chair. Not being able to hold it back any more, Papi walked towards the bed and grabbed both of Mo's feet. Using the heel of her feet he spread her legs wide open. The lubrication of the condom, made it easy for him to slip inside of her. For the first few seconds he was hitting her with nice long strokes. She began to throw it back from underneath so that told Papi she wanted to be fucked harder; so he did just that.

"Damn yo pussy tight!" Papi yelled out with his face scowled up.

"You like this pussy daddy?"

"Hell yeah. After this it's gone be mines." He said barely being able to speak.

"Ohh shit, ooh shit Papi. it feels so good babyyy. Oh my god it feels good." Mo moaned out. She couldn't front, for Papi to have been young, he was slanging dick like a grown ass man.

"Come ride this muthafucka." Papi slid out of her and turned around to lay down. Mo zoomed into his tattoo's and nearly lost it. She was stuck in such a trance that she stood still not saying a word. The tattoo of Nino and Cash on his back threw her for a loop. Her eyes began to water and just the thought of Papi having some affiliation with the two had her speechless.

This can't be. Wait how do he know them? She thought to herself.

"Mommy guess what?!" The door flew open causing Papi and Monique to jump.

"BJ?"

"Kamela?" Papi and Kamela eyed each other not saying a word. *This shit is crazy.* Papi chuckled to himself feeling slightly embarrassed. Kamela had called him a few times since the incident at the arcade but because of Aaliyah he would always let her calls go unanswered. He knew shit was about to get ugly. Kamela hated Aaliyah so he knew she would for sure tell her what she had just witnessed.

CHAPTER 19 *(Que)*

"Time to revisit the past"

"Fuck you want Puto?" Que answered the phone annoyed.

"You move to Brazil and grow balls I see." Mario chuckled at Que's braveness.

"Fuck you. Nigga you know I've always had bigger balls than yo mexican ass." Que taunted him. "Now what the fuck you want Mario?" Que said with much base in his voice. Que hated Mario and the ground he walked on for many different reasons. For starters, Mario is the one that paid him to blow up the Yacht for his best friend's wedding. The one thing that he hated the most was Mario was keeping his daughter from him. He paid Que ten million dollars to kill his friends and move away. Everytime Que asked about his babygirl Mario would simply say *he left her at the hospital where the Lopez's had abandoned her after killing her mother.* Que knew not to test Mario especially now because he had no one.

"We have a problem Que."

"Okay and it's your problem so why the fuck you calling me?"

"Well you know my problems are yours my boy." Mario said and chuckled. Que shook his head as if Mario could see him thru the phone. Que remained quiet and let Mario continue. Personally he didn't want shit to do with Mario. He had gotten his money and started a new life in Brazil with his childs mother and now wife.

"Some new piece of shit pendejo is selling coca in my fucking city. He no buy not one pinche kilo from me or my workers. His name is Papi and I need you to handle this shit rapido Quintin.

Either he buys from me or he dies." Mario spoke with force then hung up not giving Que a chance to respond.

Que shook his head still annoyed but at the same time he was puzzled as to whom could have had enough balls to come to Miami and set up shop. Even though Que had moved away to an entirely new country, he still supplied Miami and a few more states. Que was so paid that he didn't have to lay a finger on the product; just simply collect his money. Now he was upset to hear the new person had came in and not cop from him. *Fuck Mario* was his thoughts, he would find out who this person was because Miami was his city and had been since he worked for Ms. Lopez.

Que rubbed his hands down his face and stood to his feet. He went to his closet and began to prepare for the long trip that laid before him. After sliding into his Jordan 12's, he grabbed his twin berettas and headed into the room to discuss his move with his wife. When he walked into his bedroom, Gabriella was sitting at her porcelain vanity brushing through hair long blonde hair. He stood at the door and watched her beautiful frame sitting in the chair. His wife was bad, hands down. Que and Gabby had been together for quite a while. She was once the girlfriend of Bronx Carter, up until she had murdered him for Que. After the murder and the explosion, Que moved into Bronx's mansion and wifed Gabriela some time later.

"You leaving Poppy?" Gabriela asked looking at Que threw the mirror.

"Yeah some shit happened down in Miami. I gotta take a flight so I'll be back in a couple weeks ma." Que sighed. Looking at him,

Gabby was able to tell he was bothered by whatever it was but she knew not to question him.

“Okay be careful.”

“I will but what's up, let me get some of that before I bounce.” He smiled seductively. Without asking twice, Gabby stood to her feet and headed over to the bed. The long silk robe she wore left nothing to the imagination. She was naked as the day she was born and that was how she often walked around the bedroom.

Que walked up to the bed and bent her over doggy style just how she liked it. Not even taking off his pants, he released his thick carmel weapon from his jeans and positioned himself behind her. He used the tip of his manhood to get her moist and once she was wet enough to slide in, he entered her juicy pussy. “Ummm Poppy.” she called out gripping the sheets. Que began to speed up his pace and the sound of her ass smacking against his thighs was the only sound that could be heard throughout the room. “Got damn Gabby! Ima miss this pussy baby.” Que yelled out grabbing her hair. He wrapped it around his hand and used it for guidance. Gabriela was a stone cold freak so the more he pulled the more she was turned on. “Oooh shit ma I'm bout to cu...Im bout to cummm!.” Que yelled out not being able to last a second longer. Within seconds he shot his hot liquid into her pussy then rolled off her breathing heavy.

After catching his breath he rose to his feet and headed into the master bathroom to wipe himself off. Once he was done, he kissed Gabby who was still laying on the bed and told her he would see her soon. He left the room and headed down the hall because his work at home wasn't done. He turned the knob on the door letting himself in. Keisha was so busy into her novel that she hadn't even noticed him walk into her bedroom. Just like he had did Gabby, he stood back and watch his baby mother laying across the bed looking like a chocolate goddess. She was wearing some yoga tights and a crop top to match as if she had just got done working out. Her fat ass sat up perfectly off the bed making Que lick his lips. He was ready to dive in.

"Keisha, a nigga gotta hit the states for a couple weeks ma. Take that shit off and let daddy hit that pretty pussy."

"Nigga you betta go fuck yo wife." Keisha barked. Unlike Gabby, Keisha wasn't pressed at the fact of Que having his cake and eating it too. When Keisha agreed to move to Brazil, she thought that her and Que were gonna start fresh and be together but Que had a surprise for her. When the plane landed, Gabriela was the one that picked them up at the landing lot. Keisha looked at Que puzzled and shook her head. She knew it was to good to be true but because of everything she had put Que through she went along with the stay.

Back in Miami, Keisha had began to abuse drugs. One night she passed out off the white substance and their daughter had gotten a hold of the plate. When Que came in he was furious. After taking Qui to the hospital authorities had taken Qui into foster care and Keisha had disappeared. Que was in a rage and had promised himself the moment he found her he would kill her. After some time of Keisha missing, Que began taking the proper steps to get his daughter back. Keisha had finally reached out to Que telling him she was in rehab. Knowing he was the reason she had turned to drugs Que forgave her and went to the facility. Weeks after the visit, they had gotten their child back and was on the next thing smoking to Brazil to live well off. Little did Keisha know, Que was running from demise.

"Come on Keish, you know a nigga love this pussy." Que pleaded. Keisha sighed out loud in annoyance but stood to her feet to prepare to break her baby daddy off.

Everybody that knew Que, knew when it came to the ladies he was the man. Though he was now much older, he still possessed the same sexy traits he once had. His caramel skin hadn't aged one bit and his body was still ripped. His waves were still intact and the only difference was the patch of greys in his now full beard. Que drove the women crazy even Cash Lopez. Him and Cash had a love affair going on for some time until she met Nino. Que was devastated. He loved Cash to death and to this day he would never love no women like he loved her. He also loved Breelah and wanted to remain in her life forever but she too was on the ship that he had blown up so he had to put her into his past just as he did Cash. They both were now dead so he moved on with Gabriela and Keisha and that's how things would be for the rest of his life; or so he thought.

CHAPTER 20 *(Monique)*

"I'm really feeling you Papi and I hope that this won't interfere with us."

Monique stood in the middle of her bedroom floor puzzled as to what was going on. She looked from Papi to her daughter shouting down each others throat. She knew that there was possibility of the two knowing each other but messing around was something she didn't expect. Time and time again she asked Kamela was she sexually active and each time Kamela would lie. Little did she know, her daughter had slept with half of boys and men in Miami. A few weeks prior to today Kamela had finally introduced a guy to her mother as her boyfriend. Mo wasn't upset, in fact she had welcomed him with open arms. He was a nice young kid who seemed harmless, however she wouldn't let them occupy Kamela's room with the door closed.

"So now you fucking my mother?" Kamela yelled at Papi.

"Man come on with that shit. How the fuck was I supposed to know this was your mother." Papi said standing to his feet. As horny as he was he had lost his urge for sex. "Man I didn't know this was yo moms. What the fuck you doing?" Papi asked Kamela who now had her iphone in her hand and appeared to be recording. Papi shook his head and continued to dress.

"Mela baby he didn't know you were my daughter." Mo spoke still shook up. One would have thought she was shook because of what transpired at the moment but she was actually out of bewildered because of the tattoo on Papi's back. All though she didn't have time to read the writing, the portraits of Cash and Nino was clear as day. Hearing Kamela yell out BJ, it all began to make sense. Monique had attended the services for the Lopez family and even Nino's. It never actually dawned on her that Pedro and the child weren't in attendance. They never had a service, or at least she never heard of it.

The sound of the slamming door broke Mo from her deep train of thought. Kamela stood with her arms crossed over one another but didn't utter one word. She mean mugged her mother but Mo had bigger things on her mind; she was fucking the son of Cash and Nino Carter.

"Leave him alone ma!" Kamela's eyes were filled with tears. Kamela loved Papi and was hurt when he played her to the left for Liyah. She tried reaching out to him by going to his beach house but he was never there. Over and over she had asked Cali where was BJ but he would always say "He moved away." so eventually she gave up.

"I'm not leaving him alone Kamela. I'm sorry but I like him and I wanna be with him. It's not like you fucked him anyway." Mo challenged waiting for Kamela to slip up. She watched Kamela's body language and it told her just what she had wanted to know; her daughter was indeed having sex. "I can't believe you!" Kamela cried out and stormed out the room.

Mo walked over to the dresser and retrieved her phone. After dialing a number she waited patiently for an answer.

"Whats up hoe?" Arcelie answered on the fourth ring.

"Bitchhhhhh, I got some tea for that ass." Mo squealed into the phone ready to drop her bombshell.

***

The next day….

Mo woke up bright an early to begin her day. She went into the restroom to handle her hygiene then headed into her kitchen to make herself a cup of coffee. She felt bad about what happened yesterday but what was understood didn't need to be explained. Mo was in it to win it. Now finding out who Papi was made her fall more in love with him. She knew he was rolling in dough, and she had to have him. His age wasn't a factor because everything about him was grown. From his swag to his pockets and she knew Papi was now the man. She had been lonely for so long she was gonna make Papi hers and not even Kamela would stand in the way of that.

Monique headed into Kamela's room to apologize about what had happened. When she walked in Kamela wasn't inside so she searched the entire house. Coming up short, Mo sent Kamela a text ordering her home. Afterwards she sent Papi a text.

Mo: *Hey I just wanted to say sorry about yesterday. I really didn't know but this won't change anything. I'm really feeling you Papi and I hope this won't interfere with us.* A few seconds later, Papi replied.

Papi: *Nah sexy, I ain't tripping if you ain't. And good morning to you too. Lol*

Mo: *Sorry. Good morning baby. Can I see you today?*

Papi: *Yeah I got shit to handle right now but what you got up today?*

Mo: *Well right now I'm going to the shop. I should be finished there about five so I'll call to see if your busy.*

Papi: *fasho Mama hmu*

Smiling from ear to ear, Mo was happy to keep her position in Papi's life. She couldn't let him go and especially now after finding out whom his parents were. She walked into her bedroom and headed for her shower. She was gonna dress to impress because she wanted to please Papi. *it's gonna be a long day.* She smiled.

***

Four clients down, Mo was already tired. Periodically her and Arcelie gossiped about Papi but because it was packed they couldn't waste time gossiping. It was now three o'clock and Mo had been stalking the time. She couldn't wait until five to call her new boo.

"Damn who's that?" She heard a client yell out and looking towards the door. It was as if all the women in the salon heads had turned, and being the thot Mo was, she quickly ran from around her station to take a peek at what held everyone's interest. The wide smile crept across her face at just the sight of him. He stood there looking good as ever. His locks were down in the back with the top pulled back. *Damn he look just like Nino.* Mo thought to herself. Her love box was jumping at just the sight of him. He stood still and watched Mo with a cocky smile because he knew she was surprised to see him. He was rocking a pair of stone washed Jeans with a white V neck that hugged his biceps perfectly. Because his shirt wasn't oversized, it exposed his Louis Vuitton belt. On his feet were a pair of LV sneakers to match and they looked like they cost a grip. His *Papi* pendent he had just copped rested perfectly on his shirt and the diamonds were like looking at a moonlight.

"Damn can daddy get a hug?" Papi smirked. He loved the fact that Mo was nearly twice his age but submissive to him. To Papi, Mo was the baddest bitch in Miami and he could really see himself rocking with her the long way. He knew it was wrong, and he loved Liyah but he was growing tired of not being able to hold her at night. He loved Aaliyah and she was beautiful hands down, even more pretty than Mo but Mo's entire swag was to die for. She had her own business, she matched his fly, she had her own condo and he was more than sure that was her baby blue Maserati parked out front; she was on her grown woman shit. Now don't get it twisted, Papi wasn't never leaving Liyah alone. That was his baby to the death of him but right now he was exploring his options.

"Hell yeah daddy." Mo smiled shyly and ran over to hug him. She wasted no time because she wanted to let all the thirsty hoes inside of the shop know exactly who he belonged too.

After a nice tight hug, Mo broke the embrace and stood back to look at him. She was blushing so hard, her cheeks were rosy red and she was sure everyone in the shop noticed.

"What are you doing here?"

"Shit I got done sooner than I thought. Why should I leave?"

"No." Mo quickly answered making Papi chuckle.

"You look nice Mama." Papi said making her blush harder than she was already.

"You looking good too."

"Hey Papi." Some chick walked by smiling all in his grill. Mo instantly became jealous eyeing the girl with much hate.

"Sup MeMe." Papi politely spoke then quickly focused back in on Mo. "Stop tripping ma I'm here for you right?" Papi grabbed her chin to make her look at him. "Right?" He asked again for reinsurance. With puppy dog eyes, Mo simply nodded her head yes. He sensed the anger in Mo's face and he didn't want anything to ruin the moment, however he did find it cute that she was already acting out in jealousy. All that did, was told Papi that she was feeling him and that was another bonus in his book.

The sound of Papi's ringing phone made them both look down. Now Mo prayed he wouldn't have to leave. Just looking at Papi she knew he had some sort of hustle going on and of course because of his background, she would bet her life on it.

"I gotta take this ma. But get yo shit, we bout to roll out." Papi said then answered his phone. *You ain't gotta tell me twice.* Mo thought and walked off towards the back to get her bag. She would also stop by and hand Arcelie the keys to lock up. She was so happy she was nervous. Just looking at Papi she could tell he was feeling her, and the feelings were mutual.

CHAPTER 21 *(Aaliyah)*

"I wish I never met you..."

Aaliyah walked around the mall in search of the perfect dress. Her prom was a week away and she wanted to look good on the arm of Papi. He had finally agreed to go, only because Liyah kept threatening to go with someone else. As crazy as Papi was over Aaliyah she knew he wouldn't allow another guy accompanying her out so he agreed. He also gave her the money for her dress, shoes and hair even though she didn't need it.

"This the one Vee." Aaliyah looked over at Venicia whose face was scrunched up. "What's wrong?" Liyah asked concerned for her friend.

"I don't know ma. I feel sick."

"Okay well let's get this dress and we could go." Aaliyah said and pulled the dress off the rack. When they reached the register, the girl smirked at Aaliyah but she payed it no mind. She was used to that and she was more than sure it was because she was Papi's wifey. Aaliyah pulled out the 5,000 dollars Papi had given her but making sure to flaunt the huge diamond ring. She peeled off the thirty nine hundred, paid for the dress and waited patiently for the woman to bag it up. The way Vee was looking, Liyah chose to just wait to buy her shoes.

Driving down Lincoln Rd Liyah swopped up into CVS parking lot and parked. She told Venicia she would be right back and quickly hopped out of the car. The moment Aaliyah was out of sight, Venicia, opened the car door and threw up her entire insides.

She was in so much pain that she began crying out. Once she was done throwing up, she closed the door and laid back in the seat. After about fifteen minutes, Liyah came back out carrying a bag full of items. She tossed the bag over to Venicia and started the car to drive off. Vee opened the bag and began examining the contents inside. There was soup, crackers and two pregnancy test. Holding the test in her hands she looked over at Liyah and smirked.

"What bitch?" Liyah laughed out.

"For real Liyah?"

"Yes. I'm not dumb Venicia and stop being so naive. Yo ass is pregnant and we need to find out before it's too late."

"Oh my god what am I gonna do if I am?" Vee began to cry.

"Well for starters you could tell Cali and see what he say. Just because you might consider getting rid of it, he might not want that and you should give him a say so."

"True but fuck him Liyah. How about we just don't tell him period." Vee said back in her seat and began to pout.

"Well we gotta find out first." Liyah smirked and turned up the music.

***

Aaliyah and Venicia walked into Venicia's house tired from a long day of shopping. The two headed to Vee's room to put their bags down. Vee wasted no time going into the restroom to take the test so Aaliyah took a seat on her bed to wait patiently for the results. She pulled out her phone to call Papi, because she was starting to miss him. It had only been a day since they were together and she knew if she didn't see him tonight, then she might not be able to see him for a few more days. She dialed Papi's number and waited for his sexy voice to grace the phone but to her surprise she got no answer. She called back again and got the same results. After she realized he wasn't gonna answer she went to instagram to see when was the last time he had posted a pic. The moment she opened her page there were notifications awaiting her. When she clicked onto the video that she was tagged in five times her heart fell into the pit of her stomach. It was a Live Instagram video that was posted yesterday. She watched as Papi stood naked in the room with Kamela and a lady who was also naked but covering her body with a sheet. Papi began dressing and when Aaliyah heard "I didn't know this was yo moms" she clutched her mouth to keep from screaming out. The tears began to pour down her face as she shook her head from side to side. The door to the restroom opened and Venicia walked out with a tear stained face. She looked at Aaliyah who was now crying hysterically.

"What's wrong Liyah?" Venicia asked forgetting about the test that she had took that read she was indeed pregnant. Aaliyah handed Venicia the phone and the video replayed. Venicia's mouth hung open as she watched the video twice. She shook her head and fell down to her bed beside her best friend and pulled her into her arms. This had to be the worst day for both of them.

After the two of them cried together, they gathered themselves to speak.

"So what you gonna do Liyah?" Venicia asked with concern.

"It's over Vee. I can't be with him any more. I just can't." Aaliyah began to cry again. She picked her phone up off the bed and began to text Papi.

Aaliyah: *I swear I hate you. It's over hoe! Lose my fucking number and don't say shit else to me Brooklyn.* After a few seconds, Papi replied.

Papi: *man what you talking about Stink?*

Aaliyah: *Fuck you! I WISH I NEVER MET YOU!*

Aaliyah dropped her phone into her purse, she had nothing to say to him ever again in life. She was hurt. No pain on earth felt worse than the pain she felt at this moment. She looked down at her ring and it made her cry out more. *This ring is a promise that I'll be here forever. I don't give a fuck what we go through ma, you'll always be my stinka baby.* His words played over and over in her mind and everything he said was now out the window.

"So what you gonna do Vee?" Aaliyah asked her friend who was in deep thought.

"I don't know. I mean I can't have no baby Liyah. I'm about to graduate then go off to school.

"I say we go pay his ass a visit. The way I'm feeling right now I'm liable to help you kill his ass." Aaliyah said and they both chuckled.

"Let's do it." Vee said and lifted off the bed. Aaliyah sighed out and also stood to her feet. She prayed Papi would also be with Cali so she could give him a piece of her mind. Aaliyah and Venicia headed out the door but making sure to grab any weapons that they could find. Shit was about to get real because once they were done, she would be making a surprise visit to Papi's mansion.

***

Pulling up to Cali's crib that he shared with his brother Young, Aaliyah and Venicia watched the house closely. Cali's car wasn't in the driveway as usual so they figured he wasn't home. They pulled out their phones and began going through their social medias to kill time. They knew sooner or later he would be pulling up and they were gonna wait, even if it took all night.

An hour later, the sight of headlights were slowly approaching Cali's house. The car passed by Aaliyah's car showcasing it was Cali. "There his ass go." Venicia said and reached for the handle.

"Wait is that…

"Kamela!" Venicia shouted out cutting Aaliyah off. Cali and Kamela exited the car with two bags that contained trays of food. They walked up to the porch but Venicia would make her presence known before they entered the home. She jumped out of the car. The sound of the door slamming made Cali and Kamela look up. Aaliyah stepped out and followed her friend.

"So this yo bitch now?" Venicia screamed down Cali's throat.

"Gone with that shit Vee." Cali said annoyed.

"Don't tell me gone nigga. Answer the question." Vee barked. Kamela stood still with a smirk on her face looking from Aaliyah to Venicia.

"Bitch what you smirking at. I owe you a ass whopping anyway." Aaliyah ran up on Kamela and began pouncing on her. Aaliyah wasn't the type of chick to be fighting and acting rachet in public but she knew how to throw down. When she was younger her grandfather made sure to keep her in sports and most important she had a paid boxing trainer.

"Let her up Aaliyah!." Cali yelled out dropping the bags that were in his hands.

"Fuck that bitch! Fuck her up Liyah." Venicia ran up on Cali and began swinging on him. Cali blocked every shot then grabbed Venicia's arms.

"Man what the fuck yall doing?" Young came running from inside the home. He snatched Aaliyah off of Kamela who was screaming to the top of her lungs. Venicia who was now out of breath had finally let up off Cali.

"Fuck you Cali. and I hope you ready to be a daddy bitch!" Venicia yelled out through tears. Cali froze in his spot and he didn't know what to say. He looked at her stomach but it hadn't even grown yet. Many times, Cali had been ill but he didn't know why; now it all made sense. "So you out here doing all this thot ass shit pregnant Vee?" He tried to flip the script.

"Fuck you nigga! Let's go Liyah." Vee said and grabbed her friend who was still trying to get to Kamela. Aaliyah was furious. She hated Kamela for many reasons.

Walking to the car, Vee turned to look at Cali one last time. He stood stunned at everything that transpired. It was like his heart was crying out for Vee but she didn't give two fucks. In all honesty, Cali loved Venicia, but he just wasn't ready to settle down. Now that he knew she was pregnant, he wanted to run after her and tell her how he really felt but he knew it was too late.

CHAPTER 22 *(Brooklyn Jr. aka Papi)*

"When the world is on your shoulders, just push it right back."

"I don't know what is it about you but a nigga feeling you mama." Papi spoke to Monique who was sitting across from him in his restaurant. Mo was happy that Kellz wasn't there so he wouldn't blow her cover. She knew that Kellz ran the restaurant but she always made sure to keep her distance. Looking at Papi, she assumed the restaurant was passed down to him because of the royal treatment he was receiving.

"Is that right? So what you gonna do with me?" Mo said then took a hit of the *sex on the beach* hookah. Papi stroked his chin not sure as to what he wanted to say. He watched her with much fire in his eyes. Her straightforward attitude and the way she played in her hair had Papi ready to bend that ass over, right on the fluffy pillow they were occupying.

"You gone be my bitch." Papi said and turned his head trying to avoid eye contact. He really wasn't sure as to how she would react, he just prayed he wasn't jumping the gun.

"So what about yo bitch Papi? I mean I'm not tripping off her right now, but what happens when I start catching feelings for you."

"My bitch is not your concern, let me deal with that. And as far as you catching feelings, you gone do more then catch em, Ima have yo ass catching em, throwin em, leaping over them bitches, hahahah."

"You're so cocky with yo sexy ass. Hahaha." Mo laughed amused by not only his cockiness but his straightforward attitude.

“Mr Carter, here's your Lobster and garlic butter rice. And Mamm heres your order. Can I get you guys anything else?” The waiter asked politely.

“No Frances thank you ma.” Papi said and smiled.

“Get Frances beat up.” Mo laughed with a steady smirk.

“Hahaha nah ma. Stall Frances out.” He chuckled. “You ain't….” Papi was cut off by the vibration of his phone ringing on the table. When he looked at the message it was from Aaliyah.

Aaliyah: *I swear I hate you. It's over hoe! Lose my fucking number and don't say shit else to me Brooklyn.*

Papi read the message three times before replying.

Papi: *Man what you talking about Stink?*

Aaliyah: *Fuck you! I WISH I NEVER MET YOU!*

Looking over the message, he became a bit on the edge. He was curious to why she was tripping but he knew whatever it was, she was mad.

“Something wrong babe?” Mo asked knocking him from his thoughts.

“Nah ma. I'm straight.”

Wrecking his brain, he couldn't figure out what he had done. He was sure she hadn't seen him with Mo and he hadn't been intimate with any other women. *Kamela!* He thought to himself remembering the bitch was recording the day she walked in on him and Mo. *Fuck!* He cursed himself quietly. In all honesty, Papi was now sick to his stomach and had lost his appetite. He hated when Liyah was mad at him.

"We could leave if you have to go Papi." Mo said hoping they didn't have to end their date.

"You good babe. So tell me a little about yourself." Papi tried his hardest to change the subject.

After the two ate, they headed outside so they could finish talking and getting to know one another. Papi, who had Aaliyah on his mind was trying his hardest not to stress out. Meanwhile, Monique, was still in shock that she had bagged Cash Lopez's only son. No lie, Mo was feeling Papi, but she now wondered was it *a money bag lust*. Mo wouldn't mind being with Papi, and she also wouldn't mind getting a hold of his bankroll. All night she laid in her bed wondering if she could get a hold of Papi's fortune. She knew the Lopez's were rolling in dough, so she knew there had to be a stash tucked away tightly. Mo fantasized about not having to work ever in life. Though she was paid, she wasn't nearly rich as Papi. Papi watched Mo as she contemplated and admired her structure. She was bad. His phone alerted him he had a text but out of guilt, he was to afraid to look down. Building up courage he checked the message and to his surprise it was Cali.

Cali: *Man shit just got wild my nigga. Aaliyah and Venicia came over wilding out. Beat up Kamela and all that. Smh*

Papi: *wtf! I'm on my way man*

Cali: *yeah my nigga, whatever you done, Aaliyah tripping. She was screaming all types of shit about a instagram video and some more shit.*

Papi: *aight here I come*

"Aye ma. We gotta roll." I'll get up with you tonight , if that's cool?"

"Its cool and yes I'll be waiting for you." Mo smiled to insure him she wasn't tripping. The two walked hand and hand to Papi's Bentley and he opened the door for her to get in. Once she was in her seat, he couldn't resist. He bent down and placed a sensual kiss on her lips. Mo grabbed his face into the palm of her hands, and explored his mouth with her tongue. Threw his jeans, Papi, could feel his dick throbbing. The vibration of his phone broke the kiss and he quickly pulled back. He didn't bother to check it, he shook his head and walked around to his side and hopped in.

***

Instead of Papi going to Cali's, he headed to his aunt's house. The moment she let him in, he walked straight to the sofa and slouched down feeling like he had the world on his shoulders. For the first time in his life, things were beginning to take a tole on him. His baby was tripping, he was feeling Mo, he had to focus on the drug game and not to mention he wanted to finally start digging up dirt on the muthafuckas that killed his parents. Papi missed his Papa and felt like he wanted to break down. *When the world is on your shoulders, just push it right back Papi.* Pedro's words played in his mind, he wished it was that simple.

"What's wrong nephew?" Breelah said taking a seat next to Papi.

"Man aunty, shit crazy." He went on to tell his aunt everything that happened from when Kamela walked in on him and her mother. By the time he was done, her mouth hung to the floor.

"So do you like this new chick?"

"I mean. I love Liyah TiTi but she still young. Her family shelter her and a nigga hate not being able to be with her when I want to. The new bit..I mean chick, she cool as fuck and more on her grown woman."

"Well let me tell you this Papi, don't fuck up your whole life for one night. You and Aaliyah have built a great bond and relationship. What if the new chick not really what you want and you lose Aaliyah? You gotta think wisely."

"Have you ever been in love?" Papi asked Bree but already knowing the answer. Pedro had told him all about the love she shared with Que but he wanted to hear for himself.

"Yess!" Breelah beamed. "Oh my god, he was a total player but he treated me good. He did somethings that I didn't approve of, but I was madly in love with him. I made one mistake and it messed up our entire relationship. Now here I am lonely and wishing I could just go back in time. I would do things differently." Bree began to get sad just thinking of Que.

"Have you tried to reach out to him?" Papi asked in hopes he could possibly find Que.

"It's like he vanished off the face of the earth. I'm pretty much over it now nephew." Bree sighed at the lie she just told. Many nights Bree cried herself to sleep. She missed everyone, Even her sister in law Cash. When the ship blew up, she was pregnant. She wished her baby had a chance to survive, so that she would atleast have a part of Que in her life forever.

"Pack yo shit aunty. You coming to stay with me." Papi stood to his feet. Breelah looked up at him and because of the serious tone, she knew he was dead ass. When she didn't respond, he walked to the door and headed out into the nights air. Papi had a lot of his mind and it was now time to get shit in order.

CHAPTER 23 *(Brooklyn Jr. aka Papi)*

"Grand Opening."

It was the night of Empire's grand opening and shit was about to be lit. Papi had the perfect outfit and the flyest bitch was gonna be on his arm tonight. Yes, Monique was accompanying him to the club's opening; who better than the flyest bitch in Miami? Papi told her the moment she asked to go. Over the last week, he had called Liyah numerous of times, but his calls went unanswered. After trying over and over, he had finally given up. He wasn't about to keep chasing her. It wasn't like he could show up at her home, so he had no choice but to give up. As bad as he wanted to, he decided against it, not knowing how her grandfather would act out and he would hate to body his girls G Pops. Papi hated the fact that his baby was mad at him, but with Mo in the picture he was content. Since their date, they had been pretty cosy. He'd spent the night at her home several times and they'd talk on the phone all day when Papi wasn't busy. He loved how Monique made time for him, and he also loved the attention she was giving him. Papi learned so much about the beauty from her favorite food to her family history. Talking to Mo was like a breath of fresh air for the young thug. It kept his mind copacetic, something like how Aaliyah had at one point.

Cali: *Nigga you ready for tonight?*
Papi: *Hell yeah. Shit bout to be lit*
Cali: *you bringing yo knew bitch?*
Papi: *Nigga you bringing her daughter? Lol*
Cali: *Lol*

Papi broke out into a laughter reading him and Cali's text.

When Papi finally headed over to holla at Cali, Cali came clean about messing with Kamela. Papi wasn't tripping because Cali was his boy but not only that, he didn't give a fuck about Kamela. Infact, Cali had helped him out because he wanted to get closer to her mother. He didn't need Kamela feeling uncomfortable and blocking his shot. Everytime Papi was at Mo's house, Kamela would shoot him fuck faces as if she didn't care about Cali or her mother. As bad as Papi wanted to creep in her room, he ignored her and would keep it pushing. It was something about the thrill of fucking a mother and daughter that he knew he would get a kick out of, but he chose against it. He really didn't need the drama, and not to mention Mo had some fire pussy and a cold head game; Kamela wasn't fucking with her mother by far.

***

"Club Empire"

Papi stepped out of his Maybach Landaulet feeling like the man. The driver opened Monique's door and she to felt like couldn't no bitch in the club fuck with her. She was wearing a sexy sheer dress designed by *Jaydin Divine*. It was knee length and the entire front was sheer nude. It had a flowered embroidered print that trailed down the front to only cover her nipples and crotch. The moment she stood in front of Papi he eye fucked her somthing serious. When he noticed she wasn't wearing panties, his dick rose in his slacks and stood at attention. *Damn.* he thought biting down on his bottom lip.

"You getting fucked tonight mama." He whispered seductively in her ear. Monique smiled shyly but kept a straight face. There was paparazzi everywhere and she did not want not one ugly moment on camera. As the two walked towards the entrance, they posed for a few pictures then made their way inside.

When walking into the dimly lit club, the Dj was spinning Gutta Gyrlz hit song "Bag'd Him". Everyone on the dance were jamming and even the aisle ways were crowded with people. All eyes and attention stopped to watch the Boss himself. He was looking good in his two piece Armani suit that was made as a replica like one his father had in the closet that him and Cash shared. His jewelry was shinning as bright as the chandeliers above and his locks were neatly retwisted , thanks to his boo Mo. Papi didn't know to many people that attended the club but the few he'd known from being in the drug game, were most likely in the VIP's. "We got the Boss man in the house Ladies and Gentlemen! Whats up Papi." The DJ announced over the mic while nodding his head to Papi. Papi threw up the peace sign, then made his way up the stairs to his section.

Walking with Monique, he couldn't help but chuckle at the many men who admired her. She snuggled closely to Papi insuring the thirsty men she was taking. They walked into the VIP, it felt like Papi was being watched. He brushed it off as if he was tripping and kept it moving into the section. When they walked in, Young's, eyes bucked at the sight of Monique. Papi walked off to stop the waitress and that was the perfect moment for Mo to clear the air.

"Whats up with you Mo?" Young eyed Monique suspiciously. She looked at him with frightened eyes but didn't utter a single word. ".

"Please Young, dont mess this up for me. I really like Papi" Mo whinned. Young's eyes widened at the thought of her really feeling Papi. He knew Mo's snakish ways and he refused to let her fuck over his nephew like she had did all the other niggas in town. "I promise my feelings are real for him. I didn't even know he was Cash's son Young. But I'm falling for him." Young gave Mo a look as if he didn't believe one word.

"I swear Mo, one wrong move and Ima blow yo weave back." Young snardled. "Like Cash should have a long time ago." Young walked off right as Papi was walking up.

"Here Mama." Papi said and handed Mo a drink of Hennessy on the rocks.

"Thank you." She smiled uncomfortably.

"Yo what's up with you ma?"

"Nothing I'm fine."

"Yeah I seen you hollering at my boy Young. I figured yall knew each other from the city." Papi fished for info.

"Yeah, I know him from around the way."

"Oh okay." He stated then began to pour himself another shot. Papi was curious to know if Young had in fact smashed Monique. If so, he wouldn't even bother wifing her. He wasn't into chicks that had been around the block. That's the same reason he didn't wife her daughter.

A couple hours of partying, Papi was on full throttle and Mo was now tipsy and feeling herself. She danced with Papi seductively and making sure to constantly kiss him. She loved the attention she was getting from the women that were hating. Every girl in the club, wished they were on Papi's shoulder but Monique was the lucky girl chosen. For some odd reason Papi kept getting a hunch that he was being watched again. He felt awkward as hell.

Young was boo'd up with some random chick but he made sure to keep an eye on Mo the entire night. Cali had finally arrived an hour ago and he too was in the face of random women the moment he walked in. Cali didn't care one bit that Monique was in attendance, he kept doing him. In all honesty, he wasn't feeling Kamela as much as he did since the day Venicia told him she was pregnant. Speaking of the two, Aaliyah stormed into Papi's VIP angry. She walked right up on Papi with a look that said *Foreal nigga.* Papi was a slight bit nervous, however, Mo challenged Liyah with a stare down. Being the petty bitch she is, Mo snuggled up on Papi to clarify she was the woman in his presence tonight. Venicia, who wasn't pressed by Cali being in the section, stood right behind her friend ready to pop off.

"Wow forreal Brooklyn?" Aaliyah darted her eyes at Papi.

"Man don't start no shit Liyah."

"What the fuck you mean? So you and this bitch a couple now? Just tell me! That's all I wanna know and I swear I'll leave you alone for good." Aaliyah folded her arms across one another as if she were demanding an answer. Papi looked her in the eyes. She was the only one that got away with talking to him the way she did. His eyes then roamed her body, and right at this moment he had missed her pretty ass so much. *She looking sexy as a muthafuccka. Damn I miss her ass.* Papi thought to himself.

"Liyah go home ma."

"I'm not leaving here without you." She winned but standing her ground. Monique was standing on the side of Papi, and she was now growing impatient.

"He ain't going nowhere with you!" Mo shouted.

"Man shut yo ass up Mama." Papi said and he wasn't playing. No one disrespects Aaliyah and especially not in front of him.

"Yeah bitch you heard him. As a matter of fact aint yo ass too old for him old hoe?"

"An maybe you're too young for him lil girl. What your Paw Paw let you out the house tonight?" Mo laughed. Aaliyah tried to throw a punch but Papi jumped in between the two.

"Man yall not about to do this shit in my club."

"Well you better tell that old bitch something." Aaliyah rolled her eyes.

"Man go to my car Stinka." Papi stepped closer and whispered into Liyah's ear. Again she rolled her eyes then stormed off.

"I know you aint about to leave me for her?" Monique whinned. Young stood on the sideline and chuckled at the show. He couldn't stand Monique and he didn't give a fuck if she knew it. Papi also chuckled but Mo wasn't a bit amused.

"Look Mama, Ima have the driver drop you off. Ima go get my other whip and Ima come spend the night with you.

"You promise Brooklyn?" Mo whinned.

"Don't call me that. An I don't make promises, but yes I'm coming." Papi kissed her on the cheek then walked her out to the car. Before he left the VIP, he laughed to himself because he and his boy both had relationship problems. Venicia had Cali hemmed up in the corner and she looked as if she was giving him the third degree. Papi shook his head and made his way out the club.

CHAPTER 24

"A Long Lost Love"

Walking outside of the club, Aaliyah couldn't help but cry. She felt so dumb and foolish that Papi had played her to the left for Monique. She vowed to herself to dig up as much dirt about Mo because she knew in her heart she was a conniving bitch. Papi was blinded by good looks, that he didn't see it. But it was something about her that Aaliyah knew was snakish. Aaliyah was happy that Papi had left with her, because, had he chose Mo, her entire world would have been crushed.

Everyday, Liyah had thought of Papi and wanted so bad to reach out to him. He had called her numerous of times but she would always ignore his call. When she heard about his grand opening, she expected to show up looking good and ignore him. When she saw him in his VIP with Mo, she couldn't let it slide so she made her presence known. After what she saw on Instagram, there was no way she could forgive Papi, but she needed closure. After tonight, she was totally through and would be looking for a new boo ASAP.

"Why you driving so damn fast?" Papi said holding his seat belt for security. He slightly chuckled but Liyah didn't find shit funny. She ignored him and kept the pedal to the metal. She didn't care that she was driving way past the limit, hell right now she didn't care about shit. She wanted to get rid of Papi and go home to cry herself to sleep; once again she felt like a complete fool.

"Man what's up with you Liyah. You roll up in my fucking club tripping but you the one ain't been answering a nigga calls and shit. I know I fucked up but you could've at least gave a nigga a chance to explain. You just shake a nigga. It ain't like I could come to yo crib ma." Papi lifted in his seat to look at her. He also looked around to make sure he wasn't being followed; Shit just didn't seem right.

***

"You got me fucked up Brook!" Liyah screamed to the top of her lungs the moment they walked into Papi's mansion. "What you love that bitch? Huh? Thats yo new bitch?"

"Hell nah I don't love that bitch. But yes that's my new bitch Liyah. I mean what I'm suppose to do? Every Time you get mad you shake a nigga. I can't come to yo fucking house or nothing. That shit ain't cool ma." Papi was now screaming. The veins that popped out his neck told Liyah he was mad as hell. The roar from his voice was loud and demanding, it made Liyah jump.

"Whats going on down here?" Breelah approached the living area.

"My bad Aunty." Papi sighed. "Man she tripping." Papi looked over to his aunt.

"Oh I'm tripping? I swear you got me fucked up. Why did you bring me here in the first place. I asked you one single question. All you had to do was answer it and I would have left you alone for good."

"Its that easy for you huh?" Papi eyed her.

"What the fuck that suppose to mean? Nigga you the one got caught by yo little bitch while you was fucking her mother." Liyah cried out. Papi rubbed his hands down his face, annoyed.

Bzzzzzz!

The sound of the buzzard caused everyone to look over. "Who the fuck?" Papi asked himself with his eyebrows raised. He walked over to the nearest buzzard and pushed the intercom.

"Sup John?"

"Mr. Carter I have a young lady here to see you."

"Who is it?"

"What's your name mamm?" Papi heard John say to whomever the guest was.

"She says her name is Mo." Papi quickly shook his head and sighed out in frustration. The look Aaliyah wore let him know shit was about to get real real. Papi had grown tired of Aaliyah's childish ass ways.

"Man let her in." Papi sighed again then walked over to Liyah prepared for what was about to take place.

When Mo walked in, Breelah who had emerged from the kitchen eating an apple, was stuck in her tracks. Mo and Bree had an immediate stair down and couldn't believe their eyes. Mo just as everyone else thought Breelah had died on the Yatch. Now she was nervous wondering who else survived the explosion. Breelah on the other hand wasn't to thrilled about Mo's presence. She knew all about "Moe the Hoe" as everyone called her. She knew every detail from Mo trying to ruin Cash's life and even her sleeping with Que.

"I know you not about to disrespect me Brooklyn!" Liyah screamed.

"Wait why is she here?" Breelah yelled also. Papi looked over at his aunt, shocked at her statement. Breelah had began to crying harder and everyone went into a frenzy. *Wait, how the fuck she know where I stay.* Papi thought to himself.

"Calm down Liyah damn. And Monique, how the fuck you know…… before he could finish the doorbell rang. Papi assumed it was John because they made it behind the gate. Because Breelah was closest to the door, she went to answer it, but still waiting for an explanation. When she opened the door she got the shock of her life. *"Que?"*

To Be Continued…..